Items should be returned on or before the last date shown below. Items not already requested by other borrowers may be renewed in person, in writing or by telephone. To renew, please quote the number on the barcode label. To renew online a PIN is required. This can be requested at your local library.
Renew online @ **www.dublincitypubliclibraries.ie**
Fines charged for overdue items will include postage incurred in recovery. Damage to or loss of items will be charged to the borrower.

Leabharlanna Poiblí Chathair Bhaile Átha Cliath
Dublin City Public Libraries

Date Due	Date Due	Date Due

D1351116

About the Author

Kevin McManus lives in County Leitrim in Western Ireland.
He graduated from University with a Masters Degree in
History and a Higher Diploma in Education in 1998. Since
then he has worked as a secondary school teacher.

Kevin has also played in many bands over the years since the
mid-eighties in Western Ireland and in Dublin and still retains
a great love of music.

Dedication

To my wife Mary for providing me with the strong support and encouragement to finish this novel and to get it published. To my mother Noreen, my father Kevin and sister Miriam, thank you.

Kevin McManus

THE WHOLE OF THE MOON

AUSTIN MACAULEY
PUBLISHERS LTD.

A CIP catalogue record for this title is available from the British Library.

ISBN 9781786121318 (Paperback)
ISBN 9781786121325 (Hardback)
ISBN 9781786121332 (eBook)

www.austinmacauley.com

First Published (2016)
Austin Macauley Publishers Ltd.
25 Canada Square
Canary Wharf
London
E14 5LQ

Acknowledgments

To inspirational music and western landscapes. To the good people at Austin Macauley for publishing this book.

Chapter I

Solstice

Wednesday, 21st December 1988
One mile outside Ballinastrad, County Sligo

As it was the shortest day of the year, it was already getting dark when Tom rolled back the sleeve of his jumper to check the time on his watch.

"Ten past four," he whispered to himself as he leaned on the grape handle while he took a pull of his fag. He finished off the cigarette with one long, last drag and threw it out the shed door onto the farmyard outside, stamping on it forcefully with the heel of his boot.

Better get on and finish the job, he thought to himself as he raised the grape, arching his strong, tall and wiry frame. He continued to clear the straw bedding and dung from the floor of the shed, placing it on the heap outside in the yard.

When the floor was clean and the work complete, Tom took the grape and placed it carefully in the corner of the shed, then closed the door securely behind him. After washing his boots clean under the tap on the wall next to the hayshed, he walked across the farmyard and looked back to ensure everything was in order and in its place.

He took pride in his work. Everybody always said that Tom Kearns was a tidy man who did a job right. He was no slacker. He could turn his hand to anything, laying blocks, plastering and carpentry work; he could even do a spot of wiring and plumbing. The locals always remarked that Tom was "blessed with great hands and a sharp mind, but it was a shame he was so fond of the drink. Ah, sure he could have done anything he wanted, but the drink got the better of him."

Since his wife died back in '73, fifteen years now, he wasn't the same. His wife Maureen had died of cancer in terrible pain. He was heartbroken, but of course never spoke of it, instead burying the pain within himself the day he buried her in the ground.

Tom crossed the farmyard and walked towards the back door of the farmhouse. He tapped gently on the glass. Mrs Mary O'Brien, a short stout woman wearing a flowery apron, came to the door.

"That's a cold evening Tom," she said. "Do you think it will freeze?"

Tom looked up at the clear starry sky, tightened up his black top coat and rubbed his hands. "I'd say it will all right, Mrs O'Brien."

"Come in, Tom. Come in and warm yourself."

"Ah … okay, so," Tom replied, pulling off his Wellingtons and leaving them in the porch on a sheet of newspaper Mrs O'Brien had left out. He followed his host into the kitchen, where he was met with a warm and comforting blast of heat from the Stanley Range and the smell of warm soda bread baking.

Mary O'Brien was the wife of John O'Brien: gentleman farmer, publican and undertaker in Ballinastrad. Tom worked on the O'Brien's farm as a farm labourer during the winter months. The pay wasn't great, but he got his meals and plenty of free pints in John's pub at night. He was good old reliable Tom Kearns, who never looked for much pay. Cash in hand and on the scratcher too, of course. He was no fool.

"Sit down there, Tom and have a cup of tea," Mrs O'Brien said as she poured him a mug of tea and brought him out a plate of soda bread, cheese and ham. It had only been a few hours since she'd given him a large feed of boiling bacon.

Tom pulled out a chair from the kitchen table and sat down. Taking off his cap, he wiped the sweat from his forehead.

It was a hardened, tired and lined forehead. He was fifty-eight now, but he had the face of a man ten years older. However, his body was fit and agile, apart from a barking cough from too many fags.

"It's hard to believe Christmas is almost upon us again, Tom."

"It's unbelievable, Mrs O'Brien. It comes around so fast; sure, the time is flyin'."

"What are your plans for Christmas day, Tom?" Mrs O'Brien asked.

"Oh, I will be at home this year. My daughter Regina is coming home from England with her husband and her kids," Tom said.

"Ah, isn't that lovely, Tom. It's nice to have company at Christmas time. Regina, God. I haven't seen Regina in years; how is she getting on?"

"She's fine. She hasn't been home in about five years. She has two boys now. I think they're around seven or eight years old. God, I'm not too sure; I don't see them too often."

"How long is Regina in England now?" Mrs O'Brien asked.

"I think she's there about eighteen years," said Tom.

"My God, eighteen years. I didn't think she was away that long. You must be delighted that they're coming home," Mrs O'Brien said as she tidied up the mugs and plates from the table and brought them over to the sink.

Tom finished his supper and at around five o'clock, he got up from the table. He knew not to outstay his welcome. Thanking Mrs O'Brien, he told her that he would be back in the morning to fodder the cattle.

He walked out towards the back porch and closed the kitchen door quietly behind him. Putting on his Wellingtons, he went out the back door and around the side of the house to where he'd parked his Ford Cortina.

A dog ran out in front of him and growled as he turned the corner and opened the front gate. Tom patted the old dog on the head to reassure him nothing was wrong.

He got into his car and lit another fag, then turned the ignition four times before the 1974 grey Cortina eventually started. It was hard starting the last day or two thanks to the cold weather and probably needed a new battery. He would have a look at it tomorrow when he had time.

Following the short journey into Ballinastrad, Tom parked outside Dolan's Pub on Bridge Street. He turned to the pubs of Ballinastrad night after night for solace, comfort and companionship. It was better than sitting at home in a lonely house that was too full of memories, emptiness and silence now.

Opening the front door of the bar, he went in and warmed himself next to the open fire, then ordered his first pint of stout from Jennifer Dolan, the publican's daughter.

"That's a bitter evening, Tom! I'd say we'll get a hard frost. They were saying on the radio that there's heavy snow coming around Christmas, but sure, they haven't a clue," she said, placing Tom's pint on the bar and giving him his change.

"You're right there—they haven't a feckin' notion. Give us out a packet of Twenty Major there too, Jennifer, good girl."

Tom took a seat at the bar and sank the pint, following it with a half one of Powers Whiskey as he lit a fag.

After spending about two hours in Dolan's, he strolled up Main Street to O'Brien's Pub at around eight o'clock to meet the boss and get his Christmas wages and a few pints on the house.

The craic was good in O'Brien's. There was plenty of slaggin' going on and Tom didn't say too much, as usual; he preferred to listen in and make a few dry comments that always got a roar of a laugh from the other regulars. Tom was quiet, a shrewd man, a listener, a thinker. He was admired by his peers as a good worker and a clever man you could always rely on. "Sure, Tom Kearns could have been an engineer or an architect if he had got the schoolin'," was often repeated around the village of Ballinastrad.

At about 11.45, Tom looked at the clock at the side of the bar and swallowed down the last mouthful of stout, then said good luck to the publican and the boys at the bar.

"See you tomorrow Tom," said John O'Brien as Tom walked out the door as straight as if he had never had a drink.

Tom stood outside and lit a fag. The footpath and road were glistening with frost. There had been a light fall of sleet earlier that was now coated to the ground and frozen firm. It crunched under his feet as he pounded them to keep warm.

He walked slowly and carefully back to his car. The car door was frosted shut and he had to give it a good pull to open it. Sitting in the car, he pulled his car keys out of his coat pocket. He turned the ignition.

There was no response. He tried it four more times. Still no good.

"Feck it," he whispered to himself.

He got out of the car, slamming the door behind him, and thought about going back into O'Brien's and asking John for a lift home. On second thoughts, he decided he wouldn't; Tom was a proud man and didn't like having to ask for a lift from anyone.

Instead, he looked up and down the street to see if any of his neighbours were in town to give him a lift the three miles out to his house. The town was quiet, but he spotted a blue Toyota belonging to a younger man that often travelled out the road to Rossbeg; maybe he might carry him if he was on the road.

Tom decided to walk out the Rossbeg road a bit. He would probably get a lift from someone and if not, sure, the walk wouldn't kill him. He'd done it many a time before.

Pulling his cap down tight on his head and buttoning up his top coat, Tom walked against the biting frosty air and looked up at the sky with the whole of the moon shining down upon him. The road was treacherous underfoot and he slipped a number of times. He walked on for about ten minutes and two cars passed him. Eventually, he thought, somebody would recognise him and stop.

He heard another car coming up behind him. Tom decided to stand out from the ditch a bit and turn his face towards the oncoming car so he could be noticed better.

The car was approaching fast behind him. It seemed to be slowing and speeding up erratically. Tom recognised the car: a blue Toyota Starlet.

He turned to wave at the car, and at that, it swerved in towards the ditch. He tried to jump out of its way, but the car rebounded off the ditch and swerved back out in Tom's direction, hitting him on his side. He fell under the car and it dragged him fifty yards down the road before the brakes screeched.

Tom could hear the car stopping and after a few minutes, the car door opening, but he couldn't see anything for the warm blood was pouring into his eyes. He heard a man's voice slurring, "Oh Christ. Jesus Christ."

But the man did not walk towards him; in fact, Tom heard footsteps walking away. He tried to speak, but was unable to get the words out. He tried to lift his arm to make some sort of gesture, but he was unable to raise it. He was starting to feel himself drifting into unconsciousness.

The car door opened, the engine started and it drove away.

The last thing Tom could hear was a gentle cold breeze rustling in the branches of the trees overhead. He felt cool drops of sleety rain on his face.

Then there was silence.

Chapter II

THE CROSSING

Thursday, 22ⁿᵈ December 1988
Busáras, Dublin

God, it's cold, Conor Doyle thought to himself as he curled his toes inside his boots trying to warm his feet. He sat on the bus watching the passengers lugging in their cases and Christmas shopping.

The seat next to him was empty; he wondered who would end up sitting beside him. He would be very fortunate to get the luxury of a whole seat to himself on the three hour journey to his hometown of Ballinastrad in Co Sligo, especially a few short days before Christmas, when over-cramped, cold and damp CIE 'luxury express coaches' were the norm.

He stared at the pretty brunette girl coming up the aisle towards him. Maybe she would be his companion on the journey home. *No. Feck it*, he thought as she went straight for the back seat.

Conor turned to the window, writing his name in the condensation on the glass. He peered out at the doors of the bus station, watching hundreds of people shuffle on to buses going to Cork, Galway, Tullamore and Limerick. His observation was brutally disturbed by the thud of a large old woman flopping down into the seat beside him. She placed luggage on the floor beside her, forcing Conor to pull his legs into the cramped space between the seats.

Conversation between Conor and his companion spewed awkwardly as the bus pulled out from the station and out of the city onto the N4 Sligo road. Conor began to regain feeling in his feet as the temperature in the bus rose to a few degrees above freezing. By the time they reached Leixlip, the woman next to him was snoring in his ear.

Conor reached into his coat pocket to take out his Walkman and put his headphones on. He drifted into a half-sleep staring out the window at the winter countryside sliding by him as he listened to the *Fisherman's Blues* album by the Waterboys.

His eyes watered from the cigarette smoke that clouded and hovered inside the coach. He was tired; he had left London the evening before, getting the train to Holyhead and the ferry across to Dún Laoghaire. When he could, he'd caught a bit of sleep on the over-crowded train and ferry.

Thousands of Irish were making the crossing home like Conor. All were eager to see welcoming parents, children, siblings and friends. They felt embittered that at the end of their short Christmas holidays at home, they would have to say painful goodbyes yet again to return to the only choice they had: a job in England. They'd had to leave Ireland, a country that had failed them.

Conor had made the move to London two years ago at twenty-five, in the summer of 1986. After leaving school, he'd gone to university in Galway to study arts. He'd worked hard at college, receiving a first class honours degree, but even with qualifications, he'd found it difficult to find any permanent, well-paid work.

He'd spent long terms on the dole, interrupted by spells in various jobs such as part-time teaching, bar work and sales. He'd found the lack of permanent work frustrating and disheartening. Like thousands of other young Irish people, his only option had been the plane or boat to Britain or America.

This mass emigration mirrored the harrowing passage of the young Irish in the 1950s. The current generation was forced to leave a country that had been raped by unemployment, corrupt politicians, the Catholic Church, lack of investment and lack of hope.

Conor had chosen to go to England, where he had many cousins, friends and former classmates already. The Irish looked out for each other over there; a strong Irish community existed where he lived in Kilburn.

He'd started out as a labourer on a building site. However, over the last year, he had moved on to become a claims manager for an insurance company. He was happy enough in London, earning good money in a secure job at last. He lived in a comfortable apartment, had a good social life mixing with old friends from home and got on well with his English co-workers. Yet he always thought about coming back home and giving it another shot.

He hoped things had improved. Coming home now for Christmas, he played with the idea of maybe finding some reason to stay around his hometown of Ballinastrad. Hey, maybe he would find that dream job opportunity at last, or that cute girl and settle down and live in a wild remote shack up in the hills raising goats and chickens and writing poetry. He smiled to himself as he thought about the idea.

The bus journey seemed to drag and drag as the bus got caught up in one congested, bottleneck town after another. The bus shook and spluttered and the radio crackled and whistled as it stubbornly refused to sit still on any radio station. The air was thick and dark with cigarette smoke.

Conor tried to look out through the condensation- and dust-covered window to figure out how many miles were left 'til he reached the nearest stop to Ballinastrad, Ballygalvin, where his father would collect him.

After three long, uncomfortable hours, the bus reached his destination and he gladly got off.

"Thanks be to fuck," he said to himself as he dived into the luggage compartment at the bottom of the bus and pulled out his bag. He closed the compartment door and waited 'til the bus pulled off, then crossed the road to Maguire's Pub to ring home.

It was four o'clock and getting dark. The streets were lined with cars as housewives did a bit of Christmas shopping and their husbands took the opportunity to sink a few pints in the local pubs.

Conor walked in the front door of Maguire's. The small pub seemed to be stuck in a time warp; it still had that 1967 look about it. It was decorated with your compulsory J.F.K. photograph on the wall over the fireplace and the Sligo Connacht champion's team of 1975 photograph framed over the bar.

A stout, white-haired and moustached bar man watched him closely as he walked in. Not that there was anything extraordinary about Conor: he didn't look like trouble. He was average-looking, average height with a slim build and tightly cropped dark hair.

11

Conor was busting after his long bus journey and went into the gent's toilet, which stank of stale beer, bleach, puke and piss. He stood alongside a thin, middle-aged man in a filthy grey suit at the urinal. They exchanged pleasantries and had a brief chat about how cold it was and how quiet the pubs were.

"Sure, it's not a bit like Christmas," Conor's toilet companion stuttered. "Ah sure, I remember this pub twenty years ago. You wouldn't get a seat in it during the Christmas time. Sure, it's all changed. I blame that bloody television, everybody stuck at home staring into it. I don't have one myself; I have no interest in it. There's nothing but a load of bollox on it anytime I see it. Anyway, they say it can give you cancer. It gives off radiation, you know," he said, pulling one last drag on his fag before throwing it into the urinal and walking out. "Good luck to ya and happy Christmas" he said as he departed.

After using the payphone in the dark hall outside the toilets to call home to tell his father he had arrived, Conor ordered a half one of whiskey at the bar to warm himself up. The conversation amongst the other customers went quiet as he stood at the bar, the way conversation often does in an Irish pub when a stranger walks in. The few lads at the bar eyed him up under the corner of their caps.

The bar had a sense of despair about it. It was dark, dingy, dirty and depressing. It was a place where men drank beer and time. The radio behind the bar blurred out some mutant Irish country dirge. The melancholy song matched the lonesome mood of the pub.

After finishing his drink, Conor decided to wait outside. He had enough of Maguire's and just didn't feel comfortable inside it, so he walked down to the corner to wait for his lift. It was now half four and a wet, grey mist was falling over Ballygalvin.

His father's Opel Kadet pulled up. His father, Hugh, got out, grabbed Conor's hand, shook it and welcomed him home. Conor threw his bag in the back and they drove out the Ballinastrad road.

"Are you home for long, Conor?"

"I'm not sure," Conor replied. "Maybe a few weeks."

"Your mother's looking forward to seeing you. She misses you a terror."

"It's good to get home," Conor said.

"How's the job in England goin'?" Hugh asked.

"It's going well. Are you busy yourself, Dad?"

"I'm not doing a lot. The carpentry work has dried up. There's no building work going on. I do bits and pieces from time to time. If it wasn't for the farmin', I don't know what I'd do and there's not much money in that game either, only feckin' hardship."

The car moved on as an awkward silence stretched out between father and son.

"Sorry I was a bit late picking you up, son. Tom Kearns is dead and I was over at his house helping to get things ready because his daughter is due home in a day or two. Not that there was much cleaning or tidying to do around the yard. Tom kept the place spotless, God rest him," Hugh said.

"Who?" Conor asked.

"Tom Kearns, from up in Shemore. Remember, he used to help us with the hay a few years back."

"Oh yeah, old Tom. He was a nice man. What happened? Was it a heart attack?"

"No. Poor bastard, he was knocked down the other night and killed walking out home from the pub," Conor's father replied.

"Jesus, who did it?" Conor asked.

"Don't know. It was a hit-and-run. The Guards are still looking for whoever did it. He was mowed out of it sometime after twelve o'clock, after leaving from O'Brien's Pub. He was out walking home on the Rossbeg road," Hugh said.

"God, that was a rough way to go. Poor Tom, the poor guy. Hopefully they get the scumbag who killed him," Conor responded.

"Well if the Guards don't get him, his own conscience will. How could you live with yourself if you left a man to die on the road like that and just drove off?" Hugh asked, shaking his head in disgust.

Eventually, they reached the village of Ballinastrad. Conor's family lived on the main street. Hugh parked in the yard at the side of their family home.

Conor felt a sense of warmth as he saw the light on in the kitchen in the back of the house. It was Christmas; it felt right to be coming here, to see his parents, to feel at home again. He was happy enough in England, but he always had emptiness inside him, a void he couldn't fill with anything. Maybe the time had come to fill that empty space.

His mother, Mary, welcomed him in with a hug and a kiss at the door. Her eyes were red and tears came into them as she held him. She had always been the more tactile and warm of his two parents.

Mary had been heartbroken when Conor had moved to England. She was always posting him cuttings from the papers of available jobs in Ireland in the hope that he might come back home and get work.

The smell of cooking flared through Conor's nostrils. After a good meal, the family sat down to a chat and caught up on the local gossip.

"I like your hair. It suits you short like that. I never liked that long hair on you. It made you look very scruffy," Mary said as she gave Conor the once over.

"Thanks, I think," Conor replied. "Have you seen Sean lately? Is he coming home for Christmas?"

"I was talking to him on the phone at the weekend. He isn't coming over this year. He's working, he's on duty in the hospital over Christmas. He said he'll be over some weekend in the New Year with Dolores and the kids." Mary looked disappointed, staring down at the table.

Sean was Conor's older brother. He was married now and living in Dublin. Conor always felt that his parents would be happier if he settled down around the area, got a good secure job, married and had a few kids himself. He often thought about that.

Realistically, though, it wasn't an option. There just wasn't any work in the area. No prospects, no hope.

Conor's home was always a happy home growing up. Especially at Christmas time. His parents were never too well off, but money was always found somewhere at Christmas to ensure that Conor and Sean were content, happy, safe and warm.

Around nine o'clock, Conor decided to go out for a few pints in the village. Ballinastrad was a typical Irish village; with a church, a national school, a few grocery shops and three pubs: Sheehan's, Dolan's and O'Brien's. He walked across the street to Sheehan's, the largest of the three.

Sheehan's had a bar and a lounge. The bar was for the auld fellas and the lounge catered for the young ones. The lounge was usually empty. Ballinastrad, like many towns in the west of Ireland, had been plundered by emigration. But now it was Christmas time and Conor hoped that there would be a good few knocking about.

The car park outside the pub was full and the place looked like it was buzzing inside. Conor entered the main door and turned left into the lounge. *'Where the Streets Have No Name'* by U2 was blaring out of the jukebox and the laughing, jeering and shouting was interrupted by the crack of pools balls crashing together. On the small stage at the end of the bar, a band was setting up their gear.

Conor recognised one of the guys lifting an amplifier. It was his old schoolmate and former bandmate Eamonn Roddy. Conor and Eamonn had played in a rock band together for a few years. Eamonn had played lead guitar and Conor had played bass. It was mainly a covers band, but Eamonn had written a few original songs.

The band had broken up when Conor emigrated. Conor hoped to get chatting to Eamonn later and catch up and tell tales about their days together playing gigs and shifting women. He struggled through the crowd to the bar and ordered a pint of stout.

"There's a seat for you now, young fella," a middle-aged, red-faced man said to him at the bar. "I'm leaving now before this racket starts. Would you look at all the speakers those fellas in that band have? Is there any need for them? Jaysus, they're going to be feckin' loud. And would you look at the state of them? Ha! I won't be here to feckin' listen to that shite. I'm off down to Dolan's. There's a great band there tonight, Willy Rogers and the Kentucky Mountain Ramblers. All the best."

"Good man, thanks," Conor replied. He was glad to get a stool at the bar.

The pints of stout went down well and the pool table was pushed away from the middle of the floor, revealing a small dance floor as the band began to play. Conor got chatting to a few of the local lads at the bar and was welcomed home and asked how long he was staying. However, much of the chat was about the hit-and-run the night before.

An hour or so quickly passed on. At around eleven, Conor was nearly thrown out of his stool by a slap on his back.

Conor wheeled around and there was his old buddy, Darragh Lonigan. Darragh was tall and strongly built with long, wavy, shoulder-length red hair. He had about three days' beard growth and a fresh looking flesh wound over his left eye. Beside Darragh was a strikingly beautiful woman, Conor recognised her immediately.

Sarah Gallagher. She was dressed in a formal navy business outfit that made her seem out of place beside Darragh's hippy look. He was dressed like your typical west-of-Ireland-bohemian-type in a brown, baggy jumper, dirty, ripped denims and a pair of ex-army boots. Both Darragh and Sarah seemed a bit worse for wear, as if they been on the piss all day.

"Good to see you man," Conor said with a wide boyish grin as Darragh grabbed him in a bear hug. "Jesus, I haven't seen you in ages. I thought you were still in Galway."

"We're living out in Rossbeg out by Lough Oughter for the last year. Fuck, it's good to see you Conor," Darragh replied in a lazy, slurred drawl. He just exuded coolness, holding himself with a self-assured and confident air. The kind of guy who didn't really give a fuck what anybody thought, he was content with himself.

"So how's your love life, Conor?" Darragh asked. "Are you tipping any skirt over there?"

"Not great, to be honest. Here and there, now and then. Sure, you know yourself. Ah, you know me, Darragh. I could never settle down—too much of a free spirit, like a free bird." Conor laughed. "You and Sarah seem nice and cosy up in the hills of Rossbeg. Jesus, Darragh, you're finally a settled man. Next thing you'll be telling me you have a steady job and you're getting married."

"That's right. I'm finally settled, a one-woman-man," said Darragh, eyeing Marie the barmaid's legs and winking back at Conor. "I'm a changed man, a reformed character. My wild days are behind me. As for the accommodation, well now, I'm not exactly living in the lap of luxury up in Rossbeg. You should see the state of the place. But it's cool up there in the wild, rugged and windy hills of Rossbeg." Darragh sang the words as if they were a lyric from a corny folk song.

"You were always the hippy, Darragh. You always ranted in college about finding a rural hideaway where you could dedicate yourself to your painting, deep thinking about life the universe, everything and rearing sheep. You were always fond of the old sheep, you old sheep-shagger you." Conor laughed as he gave his old mate a dig in the ribs. Darragh grimaced a bit. "Sorry, man, you all right?"

"Yea, I'm fine. Had a bit of a fall the other night. Slipped out in the yard on the frost on the way to the turf shed."

"Yea, I noticed that cut on your forehead," Conor said.

"Ah, it's nothing. Too much whiskey left me a bit unsteady on my feet and I fell over. It's just a scratch and a bit of bruising—it will be grand in a day or two," Darragh replied, looking a little embarrassed.

The three friends drank on, laughing and chatting about their times together at university in Galway until three in the morning. Marie the barmaid finally got fed up of them and refused them any more drink despite Darragh's attempts to charm her. Conor got up from his stool and said good luck and he agreed to call up to Darragh's house the following day.

Chapter III

Rossbeg

Friday, 23rd December 1988

When Conor woke up the next morning, he felt rotten. His head was throbbing and his kidneys felt like they were about to bust. His tongue was welded to the roof of his mouth with a sickly-tasting glue like slime. His eyes stung and his stomach was churning like a washing machine on spin cycle.

Was he going to die? He felt like it. Just too much porter the night before. He wasn't as used to it as he once was during his student boozing sessions.

After a half hour in the toilet and a bit of a wash, he made his way downstairs at about 11.30. His mother made him a slap-up, artery-hammering, fry up cholesterol special, which was washed down with a strong mug of tea and two aspirins. He began to feel almost human again, despite the cloudy and dizzy feeling in his head that made it feel like his brain was wrapped in a thick wet sock.

He sat around for a while in the sitting room talking to his parents and watching repeats of Wonder Woman and the Bionic Woman on RTE 1. Who was better looking, Lindsay Wagner or Lynda Carter? He could never make his mind up.

At about one o'clock, he decided to go for walk to clear his head. It was cold outside, but bright and fresh. The air felt clean in Ballinastrad in comparison to London.

He walked through the village, looking around. Not much had changed in the time he had been away. The houses, shops and pubs all looked the same. Overhead, he could hear the clang of the bulbs of the Christmas lights as they hit off each other in the gentle breeze. He stopped and chatted briefly to old friends and neighbours on the street, then went into Maguire's shop and bought a pack of fags and a bottle of coke.

"Well Conor, how's things? Are you home for the holidays?" Joe Maguire asked as he counted out the change from the till.

"I am, Joe. Home for a few weeks. Nothing has changed much around here."

"Well that's for sure. It's quiet about here; there's no life about the place. Half the young people are in England or America."

"They are surely. Well, it was terrible about Tom Kearns. Have the Guards found out anything about who hit him?" Conor asked, changing the subject.

"I've heard nothing new about it apart from the fact that the Guards were searching around the road where Tom was hit to see if they can find anything that might lead them to who was responsible," Joe replied.

"Well, the whole thing is horrific. Poor auld Tom," Conor said, opening the pack of fags.

"Tom was a gentleman and a great worker. Despite the booze he knocked away every night, he was always up in the morning and ready for work at 8.30. He always had work; if he wasn't helping Dan Smyth with the building work during the spring and autumn, he was on a tractor during the summer tending to hay or silage. He was working with John O'Brien on the farm for the last few months. John will miss him," Joe Maguire said as he handed over Conor a box of matches.

"Tom will be missed surely. Look Joe, I'll be off. I'll see you again." Conor said as he walked out of the shop.

After Maguire's shop, Conor's journey brought him up to the primary school where he and Darragh had gone to school together. Next door to it was the vocational school, or Tech, as it was called, where he'd spent five good years.

He'd enjoyed secondary school. He remembered the craic he'd had there with his mates, mitching classes, smoking fags in the trees behind the basketball court and the first awkward fumblings with girls behind the old prefab.

Darragh, being the son of a county councillor, had gone to boarding school in St Enda's in Ballygalvin. The Tech wasn't good enough for the Lonigans.

Conor walked on for a half hour or so out of Castlederry road. His hangover was starting to wane, or perhaps he was getting too numb with the frosty cold to feel it. He checked his Casio digital watch: it was 2.30. He decided to head back home.

After spending a few hours back with his parents, Conor borrowed his father's car and drove out to Darragh's house to catch up on the craic. As he drove out of the village, the daylight was growing faint and he could see the sun setting over the Rathalgin Mountains. He headed out the Sligo road towards Castlederry, which was only a small village with a pub, a post office and a grocery shop. In Castlederry, he turned left and drove out the Belgooley road.

It was getting hard to see, particularly since one of the headlights of the car wasn't working. The fog was brewing up around Lough Oughter. Conor almost missed the sharp turnoff for the back road up to Rossbeg, where Darragh lived.

The fog dissipated for a time as the car climbed the hilly, narrow lane. Looking down, Conor could see Lough Oughter and the surrounding valleys and hills. It was a wild, barren place, harsh but beautiful in its greyness and bleakness. He could see the reflections of the lights of Castlederry on the lake water and the lights of Ballinastrad and Clarebridge further on. The valleys surrounding the lake began to twinkle as sporadic lights of houses and cars began to ignite as dusk fell on the country.

Darragh had given Conor directions the night before in Sheehan's Pub, but they were a bit of a blur. Conor remembered Darragh telling him that the shortest way was to head out Bridge Street and out the Rossbeg road, but then there was a series of narrow lanes and crossroads that Darragh had probably known Conor would get lost on. That was the route that Darragh always took home; it was a quieter route for avoiding the Guards.

Darragh had told Conor to take a longer route along the main road, the Sligo road towards Castlederry. It was about three miles longer, but easier to find your way, with fewer crossroads and narrow lanes. Conor thought to himself, *well, if this way is direct, I wouldn't like to take the other route*, because he was fucking lost.

He remembered Darragh saying something about an old red Fergusson Twenty with one of its front wheels up on a few blocks. He was to turn left at the next junction after that. Darragh's house was the fourth on the right hand side.

After what seemed like half an hour he spotted the tractor and continued to creep along the narrow road, having to pull in a few times to let cars go by. He stopped to ask one of the drivers of the cars that he met if he knew where Darragh Lonigan's house was.

The reply was "Darragh Lonnigan, never heard of him. Oh, hold on. Is he Councillor Lonigan's son, that long, red-haired fella living next to Pat Joe Leddy's auld house? Oh, yea, go on about half a mile on this road and turn left and up a narrow lane. It's the first house on the left. You can't miss it; there's a big hayshed beside it."

The guy's directions were spot on. Conor pulled up in the rough, muddy yard at the side of the house. He got out of the car and lifted out a bottle of Powers Whiskey wrapped in a brown paper bag from the back seat of the car.

It was freezing cold. The trees swayed and bent at the front of the house as the wind began to pick up and bite. Conor buttoned up his coat and walked toward the front of the house. His Doc Martin boots squelched through the muddy yard.

He could see a light on in the front window. He stumbled across what felt like a cat as he reached out to tap the shabby front door. No reply. He knocked harder and waited again. Still no reply.

Maybe there was no one home, but the lights were on and the curtains weren't drawn. Conor peered through the net curtain. Inside he could see Sarah sprawled out asleep on a couch with a book and a newspaper lying on her stomach. He could also hear music playing.

He admired Sarah's form for a minute and then rattled the window. Sarah sat up slowly, scratching her neck and rubbing her eyes. She stood up, turned off the music and walked slowly towards the door, stopping to put her feet into a pair of boots. She cautiously opened the door, calling, "Hello? Who is it?"

"It's me. Conor".

"Oh, Conor. Come in."

The front door opened into an average-sized farmhouse kitchen. The room felt cosy and warm, with a strong smell of burning timber coming from the old, smoke-stained stove. In front of the stove was a battered old orange-coloured couch with a multi-coloured woollen throw hanging loosely over it. Beside the stove was a ripped leather armchair with black tape holding the leather together.

On one side of the kitchen sat a brown table with three chairs. The table was untidy, with dishes, mugs and papers strewn across it. To Conor's left were a sink, electric cooker and a few creaky old cupboards, which looked like they'd been there since the sixties. Two of Darragh's paintings were leaning against the wall next to a door leading to a scullery.

"Sorry, Conor. Jaysus. I was asleep. I must have dozed off reading. Come over to the fire and sit down. I'd say it's feckin' bitter cold outside," Sarah said. Conor walked towards the leather armchair. "Watch that tin of paint beside the chair. Darragh had great plans to paint the kitchen; I was nagging him to do it for months. As you can see he made a start at it." Sarah pointed to the wall beside the window. Half of it was painted a lilac colour and the rest was a dull lemon.

"He gave up after a few hours and said he had a sore wrist. Sore head more like. Well, the tin of paint is sitting there for the last two weeks. He reckons he's too busy to finish it," Sarah said, smiling.

"Darragh was never a man for decorating or DIY," Conor replied.

"You can say that again. You should see the state of the bookcase he put up in the sitting room; it's collapsed five times." Sarah laughed. "Take off your coat, Conor. Will you have a cup of tea or coffee?"

"Tea please. No sugar and plenty of milk," he responded.

"Darragh went for a walk with the dog about two o'clock. It's dark now. He should be back soon," Sarah said as she went over to the kitchen area to make the tea.

Conor stared at Sarah as she stood filling the kettle at the sink. Her long, dark, wild and wavy hair hung down her back. She was dressed in a woolly purple jumper that fell over a pair of tight-fitting, faded blue jeans. She was tall and athletic-looking, with the stature of a model. She seemed out of place in the shabby surroundings of the kitchen.

The pair chatted for an hour about old times in Galway and what each other had been up to over the last few years. At about five o'clock, Darragh walked in and stood up to warm himself against the stove.

"Conor, how are you?" Darragh roared at his old mate.

"Sorry I'm late. I got held up in Castlederry." He winked slyly at Conor, who smiled knowingly back.

"Were you boozing?" Sarah asked.

"Me? God no. I was in saying a few prayers in the church. Here, smell my breath."

Sarah moved over towards Darragh and he pulled her towards him and gave her a big sloppy kiss. "You have, you bugger. You bloody stink of whiskey."

"Ah, no, Sarah, it's communion wine."

"Well, maybe we'll all have a shot of this," Conor said, placing the bottle of whiskey he'd brought with him up on the kitchen table.

"Good man, Conor, you never let me down. Sarah, get the glasses," Darragh cheered. Sarah obediently got up and went to the cupboard.

"Well, Conor baby, how's the craic? How's it hanging today?" Darragh asked as he downed a glass of whiskey.

"Ah, I'm still a bit rough, but I'm sure I'll get over it."

"Sure ya will. You'll be right as rain after a skin full of drink tonight." Darragh laughed.

The three old friends chatted for hours. Time passed quickly and it was twelve o'clock before they knew it.

Darragh passed out on the coach. Conor and Sarah had a mug of coffee.

"So you and Darragh seem happy enough. You like it here?" Conor asked.

"Yea, it's grand. It's a bit quiet though. I miss Galway sometimes, the bit of buzz about it. It gets a bit dark and miserable here during the winter, especially when Darragh is in the pub. It gets a bit lonely. I miss my friends in Galway and Donegal. Some of the locals here are a bit weird, especially that John McKeever guy that lives down the lane. He gives me the creeps sometimes. He called up here a few nights when Darragh was out. He never calls when Darragh's here. He's a bit freaky." Sarah said as she shook herself as if a shiver had just run down her back.

"So what are your plans for Christmas day?" Conor asked.

"Myself and Darragh are going up to Donegal tomorrow evening to my parent's house. We'll probably stay there till after Stephen's day."

"That sounds good," Conor replied.

"I hope so. Darragh and my dad don't really get on that well." Sarah paused and stared into space for a few moments. She sipped her coffee and smiled over at Conor. "So how's things for you in London? Any romancing? You must have plenty of girls over there. You always had a couple on the go in college. You were a real ladies' man."

Conor blushed. "No, nothing serious. Sure, you know yourself, a bit of a fling or a shift every now and then, but nothing you could call a romance."

"Ah, that's a shame, Conor. The right woman will turn up yet."

There was an awkward silence and to break it, Conor got up and said, "God, it's getting late. I better be heading off."

"Don't be driving home. You're half-scuttered!" Sarah laughed. "Stay in the spare room and I'll make up the bed."

"Ok, maybe you're right," Conor said. "I don't think I could find my way around the roads near here. It's hard enough in the daytime when you're sober."

A half an hour later and Conor was asleep in bed in the spare room. He woke up around half two and heard Darragh falling over something in the kitchen as he staggered to bed. Conor dozed off again and woke up around nine.

It was barely light outside. He got up, got dressed and went into the kitchen. He rinsed out a mug under the tap in the sink and had two cold mugs of water. Sarah and Darragh were still in bed, so he decided to leave a note for them.

Thanks for a good night's craic and for the bed. I will see you when ye come back from Donegal.

All the best,

Conor

Oh, and have a happy Christmas.

After placing the note on the table, he went through the back door off the scullery and out into the yard. The daylight burnt his eyes. He got into the car, which was freezing.

He put on the heater and scraped frost off the windscreen, then sat in the car for a few minutes as the frost slowly melted on the windscreen. As he sat there, still half-asleep and half-drunk, he looked around the yard outside Darragh's house.

He spotted what must have been Darragh's car. The car was parked hidden in behind an outside shed. Darragh probably had no tax or insurance on it and so was hiding it away from the Guards' view, Conor thought, not that the Guards ever called up this way.

It was a Blue Toyota Starlet. One of the front headlights was missing and the wing beside it was driven in. It looked like a fairly recent bang, because grass and muck were still stuck to the side of the car. Conor smiled to himself and laughed, picturing Darragh driving home from the pub some night and getting too close to a ditch. *Typical Darragh*, he thought to himself, *doesn't give a fuck*.

Parked out at the front of the house was a newer, cleaner-looking car, a blue Ford Mondeo. *Probably Sarah's car*, Conor thought.

Finally, after five minutes, the frost had cleared from the windscreen and Conor headed back for Ballinastrad.

Chapter IV

In the bleak midwinter

**In the bleak midwinter, frosty wind made moan,
Earth stood hard as iron, water like a stone;
Snow had fallen, snow on snow, snow on snow,
In the bleak midwinter, long ago.**

Traditional, Christina Rossetti

Saturday, 24th December 1988

When Conor arrived home, it was around ten o' clock. He had a mug of tea and a slice of toast with his father in the kitchen and followed that with two aspirins washed down with two more aspirins an hour later. His head still felt muggy and he shivered as he sat in the freezing cold kitchen. He decided to back to bed for a few hours because he hadn't gotten much sleep the night before.

Conor lay in bed tossing and turning and couldn't get to sleep. He looked around his old bedroom. The walls were wallpapered with big red and blue flowers that made him dizzy as he looked at them. The wallpaper was covered in many places by posters and pictures he had collected out of music and football magazines.

Staring straight at him was a poster of Liam Brady in his Arsenal kit. As a teenager, Conor had been an Arsenal fan and he'd idolised Liam Brady. He'd gone to Highbury a few times when he first went to London, but by then he'd begun to lose interest in football.

Next to Liam Brady was a poster of the cover of Thin Lizzy's 1979 album, *Black Rose*. Conor had spent many an evening up in this room listening to *Black Rose*. He knew every song and scratch on the record. He'd often stood in front of his mirror imagining he was Scott Gorham, throwing cool shapes on stage and checking out the chicks in the front row.

Across the room was a poster of Debbie Harry from Blondie. She'd been every Irish adolescent male's dream in the late seventies.

Conor lay in bed for a couple of hours and drifted off to sleep for a while. When he woke up, he realised it was Christmas Eve and he still had a few presents to buy. He had a quick wash and borrowed his father's car to pick them up. Aftershave and a jumper for his dad, even though he must have ten bottles of the stuff in his bedroom and a necklace for the mammy.

He drove to the nearby town of Rathalgin. As he strolled around the town, the streets were buzzing, full of last-minute shoppers. In the old market square, a tall fir tree was decorated with brightly coloured lights and they appeared magical as they danced in the cold, frosty wind. Music poured out of shops; the Pogues' 'Fairytale of New

32

York' echoed across the street from a speaker outside of a music shop. It was a beautiful but poignant song that clearly evoked the joy, sorrow and desperation felt by the Irish who were dispersed across the Earth.

As Conor continued his journey through the busy streets and shops, he watched a drunk stagger by him. The man must have been in his early fifties. A fag hung out of his mouth. Oily, greasy hair was hanging lank across his forehead. His eyes were red, bloodshot tired and he was dressed in a filthy, dark brown suit. His grey tie was loosely opened around his neck and the collar of his shirt was bent up. The crumpled shirt was covered in Guinness Stains and his black shoes were worn and bleached in piss stains.

Conor thought to himself how many times he had seen such a character in Irish towns, or in Irish pubs in London. So many of the Irish that had emigrated to England in the fifties as bright, enthusiastic young men, excited to start a new life had now, thirty years later, ended up like the drunk on the street in front of him. Their life stories were etched into their faces by too much booze and fags, too little sleep, and too little hope on a path of self-destruction.

After looking through a few shops and picking up some of the presents, Conor decided to stop off in a pub for a mug of tea and a toasted sandwich to get a break from the shopping and the cold.

The pub was called O'Flaherty's and it was fairly full, as the evening crowd was coming in. Several men sat at the bar as they listened to well-dressed returning exiles telling their bullshit tales of their epic adventures overseas. A pretty blonde barmaid sat behind the bar on a stool, looking bored as she listened to the bar chat and tried to watch the Australian soap 'Neighbours' on the television on the shelf at the end of the bar.

She caught Conor's eye and they smiled awkwardly at one another. She was attractive, but it was hard to figure out her age; she could have been eighteen. Maybe older. She was tall with a slim figure. Perhaps she dreamed of being with the bronze, blond beach hunks holding their surfboards on the television. She probably would end up there someday, like thousands of others who had started new lives in sunny Australia.

The eighteen bells of the angelus rang out on from the T.V. to remind the customers and the barmaid that they weren't on a bright, sunny, sandy beach in Australia but instead in a nation choked by the iron grip of the Catholic Church. A nation that was very slowly releasing itself from the church's grip finger by finger thanks to a slightly more enlightened younger generation. It was six o'clock and time to make a move.

Conor went back out on to the street, wrapped his long black coat around him and finished off his shopping. He returned home about eight o'clock and spent Christmas Eve with his parents, even managing to drag himself up to midnight mass. This was a novelty for Conor, but it felt right being there with his family, listening to the carols and watching the young kids with bleary eyes who were dreaming about what Santy would bring them in a few short hours.

Conor always enjoyed the innocence and goodwill of Christmas. It was a time to be with family and it reminded him of the magic of Christmas twenty years ago, when he was a young lad. Christmas Eve then was full of wonder and anticipation, a bright beacon in the dreariness of Irish winter. A time of celebration, a time of hope for renewal.

Whether you were a Christian or not, the days around the Winter Solstice had been celebrated in Western Europe since pre-Christian times. It marked mid-winter for the ancient people, who had celebrated that they had survived the dark, cold season and that the days would slowly start to get longer and warmer. The light would soon return and there was hope that spring would come in a few months, and that was worth celebrating. The solstice celebration would keep their spirits, morale and strength up so they could face the last two winter months, which were usually the harshest.

Chapter V

The whole of the Moon

Monday, 26th December 1988

Around four o'clock on Stephen's Day, Conor needed a break from the reheated turkey, sprouts, ham and Steve McQueen and Yul Brynner films. You can only watch *'The Great Escape'* and *'The Magnificent Seven'* so many times. He decided to go out for a few jars and hopefully meet up with some of his old mates that might be knockin' about.

Conor headed into O'Brien's Bar. It was a small, old-style bar and there was a good crowd gathering in for the evening's craic. A traditional group played in the corner and everybody seemed to be in good form, all probably glad to get a break from the goggle box at home. Conor got chatting to a couple of lads he used to play football with ten years previous and they reminisced about past glories on the pitch and winning the junior county final against Glengarrif in 1980. The pints of stout were cool and creamy and they flowed down easy.

Time passed quickly as the conversation moved away from achievements in football to other conquests at Xanadu's Nightclub in Kelly's Hotel in Rathalgin. The lads informed Conor they had a taxi booked for ten o'clock to take them to that very fine aforementioned establishment, and they tried to twist Conor's arm to go with them to try to relive past adventures. Conor made his apologies and said he would give it a miss for now, but he might meet them there later on.

Around ten, Conor's old school mates left O'Brien's, singing '*The Boys Are Back in Town*' as they half-staggered out the door. Conor sank the end of his pint of stout, followed it with a shot of whiskey and decided to cross over to Sheehan's for a change of scenery. He went into the lounge and was surprised to see Darragh sitting up at the bar.

"Darragh, good man," Conor said.

"Conor, how's it goin'?" Darragh asked as he got off his barstool and smiled to greet his old buddy. "Will ya have a pint?"

"I will. I thought you were meant to be in Donegal 'til tomorrow." Conor grabbed the free stool beside Darragh at the bar.

"Don't mention the war. I had a big bloody row with Sarah's auld fella. He's a fuckin' bastard—I can't stand him. He doesn't think I'm good enough for his little princess. Thinks I'm a layabout and a bad influence. Well I've had enough of his shite. I couldn't bite my lip much longer and I let him have it last night."

"Jesus, did you hit him?" Conor asked.

"No, I didn't, just gave him a piece of my mind. Ended up in a big bloody shouting match. I left Donegal early this morning."

"How's Sarah? Is she okay?"

"Yea, I think so, but she's upset as fuck and mad as hell at me. She stayed up there and said she didn't want to see me again."

"God, sorry to hear that. Ah, you'll patch things up. It will work out," Conor said as he sipped his pint.

"I hope so. God, I don't know anymore—maybe I'm better off on my own. Perhaps Sarah's auld fella was right; maybe I'm just no good for her. I'm not a good person, Conor." Darragh was silent for a few minutes, staring into his pint glass and then he held his face in his hands and sighed. "I'll be back in a few minutes—I'm going for a piss," he said, getting up from his stool.

It wasn't like Darragh to get so down in himself; he usually brushed things off fairly quickly. He was taking this row very badly, Conor thought to himself.

"Anyway, fuck it. What's the craic?" Darragh asked when he returned, trying to lift the mood. "You don't want to sit here listening to me moaning about my troubles. Have another drink."

Darragh whistled over at the barmaid, Marie and ordered two whiskeys. She smiled cheekily back at Darragh.

"I think she fancies me." Darragh laughed as he elbowed Conor. "She definitely has a soft spot for me. She's not bad looking, is she? She's a fine woman."

"She's all right." Conor smiled. He was glad to see his old mate hadn't changed much since their college days.

The hours slipped by and it was soon closing time. Marie and another barman tried to clear the bar.

"One more quickie," Darragh shouted at Marie as she walked by.

"No bloody way. It's after one o'clock and the squad are parked across the road," Marie said as she swept the fag butts on the floor.

"Ah, feck it, Marie—where will we get a drink now? And it's Christmas time!"

"You can always go to Xanadu's," Marie replied, trying to get the lads off the stools so she could close up.

"That shithole? Sure, the drink would kill you in that place. It's pure slop," Darragh said as he tried to fill his pint glass by leaning over to the tap across the counter.

"Well, you might as well go home, so, because you're getting no more here. I'm locking up in ten minutes," Marie said, pulling the glass out of Darragh's hand.

"Where you going then yourself, Marie?"

"Don't be so bloody nosy," she replied.

"Ah, go on," Darragh persisted, giving his best charming grin. "Where you off to yourself?"

She burst out laughing at the silly grin on Darragh's face. "I'm going to that Xanadu's shithole, as you called it."

Darragh paused for a minute and then asked her, "How you getting there?"

"I'm motoring there myself," Marie said as she continued to pick up glasses from the tables.

"Well, fuck it, Conor, what will we do? Will we go along for the craic?" Darragh asked.

"Ah, I don't know," Conor hesitated.

"Come on to fuck! You're only young once and it is Christmas, the season to be merry," Darragh said in his best convincing manner.

"All right, what the hell," Conor replied.

"Hi Marie, any chance of squeezing us two fine lads in with ye and giving us a lift to Xanadu's?" Darragh asked.

"Well, I have to pick up two of my mates from O'Brien's. I suppose I could fit you in, boys. I'm leaving in ten minutes, as soon as I'm finished here and ye feckers get out so I can lock up," Marie said with a flirty smile.

"Grand, so. We'll meet you outside O'Brien's," Darragh replied as the boys went outside and had a quick smoke.

Marie drove up outside the pub and the lads got in the backseat. They chuckled as they watched Marie's two mates stagger out of the pub next door and get awkwardly into the car as they roared laughing. Darragh looked at Conor and winked while he rubbed his hands.

The small Mini bumped along the twenty mile journey to Ballygalvin. It was a hilly and bumpy road pockmarked with potholes and the worn suspension of Marie's small car didn't make the journey any better.

Conor could feel his stomach heaving as the car hit bump after bump. He was afraid at one point he would have to get out to puke, but fortunately he managed to hold the contents of his stomach down.

Marie parked in the car park at the back of Kelly's hotel and she and the others walked around the side of the hotel towards the entrance to Xanadu's nightclub. Twenty or so teenagers were outside the front door trying to get in, but the heavily built, bearded bouncer wasn't giving them an inch. On any other weekend night, he probably would let them in, but this was Stephen's night, the busiest night of the year and the place would be packed, so he could be choosy about who he decided to allow in.

As Conor and his companions queued up to pay, they could hear Culture Club's *'Karma Chameleon'* playing, followed by Dexys Midnight Runners' *'Come on Eileen'*. Conor hoped that the DJ wasn't going to play shite music all night.

He paid his fiver to a grumpy middle-aged woman at the door and hung up his coat in the cloakroom, then went for a quick leak in the gents along with Darragh before heading to the bar to get a pint of slop. They wouldn't chance the Guinness, instead ordering two pints of what was supposed to be Harp lager. However, it looked a very dark brown colour and had a warm, soft and slimy taste. God knew what was mixed through it.

Conor took a mouthful and cringed as he swallowed it. "Jesus, this stuff is rotten. It's fuckin' vile."

"Yea, I know, it's desperate piss. I told you this place was a shithole," Darragh replied as he took a sip from the pint and laughed.

The boys knocked back a few more pints of the gruel and swallowed a few shots from the top shelf to wash away the taste. They decided to move away from the bar and closer to the dance floor to check out the talent on display.

Dire Strait's *'The Walk of Life'* blared out of the speakers and the dance floor was full. The song ended and the DJ announced the final slow set of the night as he began to play *'Wonderful Tonight'* by Eric Clapton. As Conor and Darragh stood there propped up against the wall on the side of the dance floor, Marie walked by on her way from the bar.

"Well lads, how ye enjoying yourself? Ye both look a bit the worse for wear." She smiled.

"Not a loss on me," Darragh said as he jumped forward, stuck his chest out and straightened himself, in the process nearly knocking over a couple dancing on the edge of the dance floor. He jumped out on to the floor himself, pulling Marie after him. "I'll show you how sober I am and wait 'til you see me moves."

Darragh gave a piss take impression of a John Travolta's dance moves from *Saturday Night Fever*.

"It's a slow set, you prick, not a disco song," Marie said.

"Grand, so. I'm a dab hand at the old slow set waltz too, no bother to me," Darragh said as he wrapped his arms around Marie and pulled her close towards him. Marie laughed and seemed to enjoy Darragh's sense of humour and charm. The pair of them stayed on the floor through the next two slow songs, Foreigner's *'Waiting for a Girl Like You'* and *'Je T'aime'*. Darragh staggered a few times and at one point, he fell over, pulling Marie down on the floor with him. She helped him up off the floor and they both laughed and continued their drunken waltz.

At the end of the dance, Marie and Darragh came over to Conor and the three of them got a seat back at the bar. They bought a few more drinks and were joined by one of Marie's friends, who was introduced as Jennifer. The four got talking and pretty soon, the DJ was playing the national anthem, which marked the end of the disco. The full lights came on and the bearded bouncer began to herd the customers out the front door like sheep.

Conor decided to go and get his coat from the cloakroom. He was about ten minutes queuing up and when he returned to the bar area, Darragh, Marie and Jennifer were gone. He guessed they must be outside at the car.

He followed the drunken crowd outside into the cold and frosty night air. He lit a fag and walked slowly towards the car park. Beside the gate at the entrance to the car park, he could see two figures slumped towards a wall. He didn't pay much attention at first, as there were countless couples in the shadows along the wall of the hotel. His fag blew out in the cold air and he fumbled in his coat pocket for matches but couldn't find any. He noticed the red butt of a fag end held in the hand of the couple at the gate and asked the guy for a light.

"Any chance of a light, buddy?" Conor asked.

He was surprised when Darragh wheeled around. He held out a lighted fag behind him and Conor noticed that Marie had her arms wrapped around him.

"Sorry," Conor said, surprised. "I didn't know it was you, Darragh". He felt awkward, thinking that he had come across something that he wasn't supposed to have discovered.

"Here's the keys to the car, Conor," Marie said. "We're going to get chips. Do you want any?"

"Yea, get us a burger and curry chips. I'll fix up with you later."

"Did you see Jennifer?" Marie asked.

"No, last time I seen her was inside in the hotel." Conor replied as he walked towards the car.

"Ah, she's about somewhere. Maybe at the chipper," Marie said.

When Conor got back to Marie's car, Jennifer was leaning against it, shivering.

"Jesus, it's fucking freezing," she said.

"I've the keys to the car. I'll start her up and get the heat going," Conor said as he opened the car door.

"Great stuff," Jennifer said and the pair got in.

Jennifer climbed into the back seat. Conor admired her as she stretched to get in behind the front passenger seat. He turned the ignition on, put on the heater and got into the back seat beside Jennifer to wait for Darragh and Marie.

"Where's your other friend that came with you? The blondie girl?" Conor asked.

"Oh, that was Patricia. She got a shift and went off with him. Where did Marie and Darragh go?" Jennifer asked, lighting a fag and rolling down the window.

"To the chipper," Conor replied.

"They are some pair, both as bad as each other. She only shifts him when she's drunk. But I think she likes him. He's going out with that snotty, black haired cow from Donegal, though. I don't like her; she's a big headed bitch," Jennifer said in a slurred voice.

Conor was, in one way, shocked to hear about Darragh and Marie's ongoing affair. However, when he thought about it, he realised Darragh couldn't have changed that much since his college days, when he would be going out with four girls in the same week, sometimes in the same night. Darragh still saw himself as a bit of a Lothario.

"What do you do, Jennifer? I mean, what do you work at?" Conor asked.

"I work in the family pub at the weekends and during the holidays."

"Do you enjoy it, bar work?"

"No, not really. Listening to old men talk about the price of cattle as they slobber over their pints. I won't be working there for much longer. I'm getting out of Ballinastrad. It's a bloody kip. I'm in second year of a Languages and Marketing Degree in UCD. Two more years and I'm off to work in Germany. I'll be out of here like a flash." Jennifer was clearly a confident girl and in her mind, she was set for bigger and better things.

Eventually the conversation dried up and they decided that the best way to keep warm was to snuggle up close together in the back seat. And when Darragh and Marie returned to the car a half an hour later, Conor and Jennifer quickly moved apart.

"Conor, you old wolf you, you can't be trusted. You're some boy." Darragh laughed.

"Jennifer Dolan, I'm surprised at you." Marie smiled as she got into the driver's seat. "The car is nice and warm and steamy. I can't see out the feckin' windows." She chuckled.

"Yea, I put the heat on to clear the frost off the windows," Conor said.

"You put the heat on all right, Conor," Marie said. "But now ye can't see out with the condensation on the windows."

The four of them laughed as they tucked into their feed from the chipper and Marie headed the car for home. She dropped Conor and Jennifer off in Ballinastrad before swinging the car around in the middle of the main street to head out the Rossbeg road to drop Darragh home. She beeped the horn as she turned the corner and Darragh stuck his head out of the passenger car window and roared at Conor, "Take it easy on that young one. I'll see you tomorrow for the cure."

Conor and Jennifer stood on the street in an embarrassed silence.

"Well, look, I suppose I might see you around," Conor said. "Sorry about Darragh. He can be a bit of an asshole sometimes."

"Ah, he's all right, he's just crazy. He's good craic, though," Jennifer said as she stared at the frosty road.

"Yea, I suppose he is," Conor replied. He couldn't think of anything worthwhile to say to Jennifer and made some daft comment about the weather. "It's been very cold the last few nights, hasn't it?"

"Yea, the road is like glass, it's so slippy with the frost. I hope Marie is okay in the car; she's a bit of a lunatic of a driver. We don't want any more people killed on the roads like poor Tom Kearns," Marie said.

"Poor Tom, that was terrible. He was a lovely man; he used to help me and my father with the hay a few years ago. I always thought that he was such a nice, quiet, gentle man and a great worker," Conor said.

"He came into our pub that night before he was …" Jennifer paused. She was almost in tears. "Before he was killed on the road by some cowardly bastard. Tom would always be in the bar early every evening about seven or eight o'clock. He would always chat away and ask me how I was, he was always so lovely and pleasant. I never seen him drunk, despite all he would drink. He was always the same, Tom. I can't believe somebody could knock him down on the road and just leave him there. It's too horrible to even think about."

"It must have been some fucker that would leave him there on the road all right. I hope the Guards get whoever is responsible soon; he or she deserves to get the book thrown at them. It was probably some drugged up scumbag low-life that killed poor old Tom," Conor said.

"Yea it probably was...... Look, I better get going. Goodnight, Conor."

Conor gave Jennifer a goodnight kiss and the pair parted. He strolled down the street to his parents' house, and Jennifer crossed the road to her father's pub, Dolan's, on Bridge Street. She let herself in through the side door and closed the door behind her.

Chapter VI

Renegade

Tuesday, 27th December 1988

Conor woke up to yet another bloody hangover.

This one was a real doozy. His head felt like he had been kicked by a horse, and his mouth tasted like he had been kissing the same fuckin' horse's arse. He tried to raise his sore dizzy head off the pillow, at the same time reaching his right hand from under the warmth of the blankets into the cold bedroom air towards the Arsenal mug full of tap water he had brought up to bed with him earlier that morning. He brought the mug towards his lips, which he could just about open with all the sticky, scummy saliva in his mouth.

He swallowed the cold mug of water and it felt good washing down his throat. He scratched his head and thought about getting up. Trying to focus on his wristwatch on the locker beside his bed, he eventually worked out that it was 11.45.

He had gotten to bed about five after falling asleep in the armchair in the kitchen after telling the family dog, Jack, that he loved him very much. Could he face another day on the beer again today?

He had made plans to meet Darragh for the cure in Sheehan's Pub at two o'clock. That didn't seem like such a good plan at that moment, the thought of it now made his stomach churn.

Eventually, he pulled himself out of bed and staggered into the bathroom, still feeling dizzy and uncertain. He threw cold water on his face three or four times to try to wake up, then went back to his bedroom to get dressed. He gave himself a spray of Lynx deodorant under the arms to keep himself smelling sweet, then pulled on the shirt, socks and jeans he'd been wearing the night before and laced up his boots. His jeans stank of beer, smoke and curry chips.

Conor pounded downstairs into the kitchen and made himself a rasher sandwich and a mug of tea. He started to come back to life, although his head continued to thump if he made any sudden movements, so he slumped in the armchair for a few hours and watched the film 'Escape to Victory' in the sitting room with his dad.

At half past two, he told his parents he was going out to get a bit of fresh air and crossed the road over to Sheehan's Pub for the cure. Darragh was already perched up at the counter.

"Good man, Conor, you're alive! How's it hangin' today, boy?" Darragh asked, slapping Conor on the back.

"Not the best," Conor replied.

"What you havin' to drink, buddy?" Darragh smiled.

"God, I'm not sure, not feeling the best. Get me a brandy and port. It might settle me."

49

"Right, good stuff." Darragh beckoned at the barman "Stick on another stout for me while you're at it."

The brandy medicine was a hard tonic to swallow, but Conor knew from experience that it would settle the stomach and the nerves and help to blow away the horrors. After sipping on the brandy for ten minutes, he was ready to chance a pint of stout.

It was hard got down and he drank it slowly, nursing it for half an hour as the brothers in arms chatted about the night before and past conquests.

"Well, how did you get on with that lassie last night? Who was she?" Darragh asked.

"Jennifer Dolan from the pub up on the road and before you ask, nothing happened. I was the perfect gentleman as usual. What about yourself and Marie? What's going on there? I heard that the two of ye get it together whenever poor Sarah's back is turned. You'll be caught out yet." Conor grinned.

"I'm a smooth operator, a cunning fox. I move in the cover of darkness, in the shadows. I'm a nocturnal beast. I can't be caught. I'm a wild thing," Darragh said as he strutted beside the counter and laughed.

One drink turned into ten and the arms on the loud, ticking clock over the bar whizzed around until it was nine o'clock and the boys were merrily jarred again. The door opened up, allowing an icy chill to enter as Sarah walked in.

Conor turned around and got up of his bar stool. "Ah, Sarah, how's it going? Will you have a drink?"

"I thought I'd find ye here. Where is Darragh?" Sarah asked.

"He's just gone for a slash," Conor responded as he smiled with bleary, burning eyes.

"Get me a vodka and coke, so, please," Sarah requested.

Even though Conor wasn't in possession of his full faculties, he could sense by Sarah's tone and body language that she wasn't in the best of form. "Are you okay, Sarah?"

"Yea, I'm … grand," replied Sarah as she gulped down a large mouthful of vodka and coke. "Well, to tell you the truth, I'm …"

Just then, the door to the men's jacks opened and Darragh staggered into the bar, taking the last pull out of a fag before discarding the butt on the floor and crushing it with his boot.

Sarah and Darragh looked at each other awkwardly. The silence between them was cold and Conor uncomfortably tried to pierce the silence by saying something ridiculous like, "sure, it's not a bit like Christmas. Isn't fierce quiet all together?"

The three friends all smiled at each other.

"Right, it's my round," Darragh slurred. "What are ye all having?"

Time slipped by as the drinks flowed. Darragh got up off his stool and swayed as he said, "Fuck it, I think I'm pissed again."

He smiled and laughed, staggering off to the jacks. He fell over a small table and stools, but picked himself up and turned around to Conor and Susan and roared laughing again.

"So, Sarah," Conor began. "How you feeling?"

"Oh, not too bad. These vodkas are hitting the spot."

The pair chatted for a time before Sarah said, "Darragh is a long time in the jacks. Maybe you should go and check on him, Conor. He could be asleep in the cubicle. That happens quite a lot when he's pissed as a newt."

"Oh yea. Suppose I better go and check to see if he's still conscious," Conor said as he walked towards the toilets.

He returned after a few minutes. "There is no sign of him in there."

"Where the feck did he go?" Sarah asked, swallowing her drink. "He could have gone for a sleep in the car outside. I'll go and check." She wrapped herself up with her long grey coat and cream scarf.

"I'll go with you. He could have collapsed outside," Conor said, laughing.

They went out the side door to the car park. It was full of vehicles and poorly lit. The night was cold and foggy.

"What kind of car are we looking for?" Conor asked.

"My car. A Ford Mondeo. Darragh has been driving it for the last few days because he got a bang or something on his own car and has to get it fixed."

After some time, they spotted the Mondeo parked in the lower corner of the car park under a tree and next to the wall of Murtagh's hardware shop. Sarah walked over towards it and Conor followed her. As they approached the car, Conor noticed that the light was on inside and the windows were covered in a white frost.

"He must be asleep inside," Conor said to Sarah as he laughed.

Sarah knocked on the window of the driver's door and called Darragh's name. She opened the door and looked inside, Conor stood behind her. Her jaw dropped to the ground as she discovered Darragh in the backseat and a girl with long brown hair lying next to him.

"Darragh! Darragh, you fuckin' bastard. How could you and with that barmaid bitch, Marie," Sarah roared.

Darragh turned around to face Sarah. "Oh fuck."

Marie stared up at Sarah embarrassingly from the backseat of the car next to Darragh.

"Darragh, you cheatin bastard," Sarah screamed. "You fuckin' dirty scumbag."

She turned around and cried loudly as she ran across the car park and back into the side door of the pub. Conor ran after her. She held her head in her hands as she walked quickly to the ladies' toilets, wailing. He stood outside the ladies' toilet and waited for her to come out. After standing there for ten minutes and feeling awkward, he went back into the bar to get his pint.

A few minutes later, Darragh came into the bar and asked, "Where is Sarah?"

"We went out to see if you were okay. We thought you might be asleep out in the car."

"No, Conor. Oh, fuck it," Darragh replied. "Sarah just caught me out in the car with that Marie one."

"I know, Darragh, ya stupid prick ya, I was standing beside Sarah. You should have been more careful. Jesus Christ, Darragh, you've fucked up now. It will take some charmin and sweet talkin' to get out of this one."

"Don't I know it?" Darragh replied as he knocked back a half one of whiskey. "Where is Sarah, anyway?"

"She's in the toilet," Conor said.

"Will you go and check to see if she is okay, Conor? Please?" Darragh asked as he lit a fag to calm his nerves.

Conor headed out toward the side door of the pub and found Sarah standing outside the toilets fixing up her make up.

"Are you okay, Sarah?" he asked.

"Yea," Sarah said. "Is Darragh in at the bar?"

"He is, yea. He was wondering where you were," Conor replied.

"Look, I'm heading home. Well, I'm actually heading over to stay with a friend in Ballygalvin. I just rang her, she's coming to collect me. I said I would meet her outside O'Brien's Pub across the road, I'm not going back into the bar to that asshole," Sarah said as she put on eyeliner with a pencil and looked into a small mirror that she took out of her handbag.

"Sarah, Darragh is pissed drunk. He doesn't know what he is doing, why don't you talk to him? I'm sure he's sorry."

"I can't believe that you are trying to defend him. Look, Conor, I don't really want to talk about it, I'll chat to you again. I better go."

"I'll walk you over to O'Brien's, Sarah and at least wait with you until your friend turns up."

"Okay, thanks," Sarah replied, taking Conor's arm as he helped her across the road.

They crossed the icy street over to O'Brien's Pub and stood outside it for ten minutes until a white Fiat car pulled up.

"There's Roisin's car now, I better go over to her. I will give you a call tomorrow. Thanks for waiting with me, you're a pet," Sarah said as she gave Conor a little kiss on the cheek.

Conor waited until the car drove off, then went back over to Darragh in Sheehan's. Darragh was sitting hunched over the counter staring into a glass of Powers Whiskey.

"Well, how is she he?" he asked.

"She's gone off to stay with some friend called Roisin. I think that was her name, Roisin or Rosey or something like that."

"Roisin Sheridan," Darragh replied. "That cow. She works with Sarah in the bank. She's a right bitch—hates my guts. She is always trying to fix Sarah up with lads in the bank. She says I'm no good for her, I'm holding her back from getting promotion. Bloody cow. Rotten bitch."

Conor and Darragh drank on as Conor tried to console Darragh and convince him that he would talk Sarah around and that everything will be back to normal in a few days. It was not the first time that Sarah had found out that Darragh was two timing her. She always took him back. She always forgave him and gave him one last chance. Darragh had an innate devilish charm, he could always win women over.

The lights started flickering in the bar to give the nod for last orders.

"It's 12.30," Conor said. "I'm whacked. I'm off to bed. Do you want to stay in the spare room in my parent's house? You're not fit to drive home and the roads are like glass." He got up from his bar stool.

"Nah, I'll drive home," Darragh replied.

"No fuckin' way, Darragh, you'll kill yourself. The roads are as icy as fuck," Conor pleaded.

The pair walked outside and Darragh slipped and fell on the footpath.

"I see what you mean." Darragh laughed as Conor helped him up. He turned and looked back at the car and thought for a moment.

"Okay, Conor," he said. "I'll take you up on the offer of your spare room. I hope your parents won't mind."

"No hassle. Come on," Conor replied as he led Darragh across the road.

The next morning, Conor woke around eleven, got up and dressed and went across the landing and knocked on the spare room door to see how Darragh was. He opened the door and discovered the room empty. He went downstairs into the kitchen and asked his mother where Darragh was. She informed him that he had got up around nine and had a cup of tea and a fag and headed over to get his car to go home.

Chapter VII

Broken Land

Friday, 30th December 1988

Conor decided to take it easy at home for a few days and give the drink a break and the liver a chance to recover. He enjoyed time spent with his family with a clear and sober head and they went on visits to friends and relations in the area.

On the day before New Year's Eve, Conor decided to find out how Darragh and Sarah were getting on. He imagined they might have patched up their differences by now. He knew that Sarah had forgiven Darragh in the past, but it would take some sweet talking from Darragh to win Sarah over this time. Finding him in the middle of the act with Marie in the back of the car must have taken the biscuit.

Conor took a stroll around the pubs in town to check if Darragh was about. He decided to have a quick pint in O'Brien's Pub.

"How's things, John? Had you a busy Christmas?" he asked.

"Yea, Conor, not too bad. The bar was busy most nights, I can't complain," John O'Brien said as he pulled a pint of stout for Conor.

"Did you see Darragh about the last few nights? Darragh Lonigan?" Conor asked.

"No, he hasn't been in here in a while, I haven't seen him in a few days. It's not like Darragh. He usually comes in for a few most nights," John said, giving Conor his pint.

"Thanks, John," Conor said as he handed over the change.

"This one is on the house," John said. "I meant to give you a Christmas drink earlier, anyway. Better late than never. Happy New Year to you."

"Thanks, good man yourself. Happy New Year." Conor saluted John as he lifted the pint off the counter.

"Yea, hopefully it will be a better year than this one. I heard that Tom Kearns's funeral is in the morning. I'd say it will be huge. He was well-known and well-got," John said.

"They were a long time organising the funeral," Conor replied.

"His body was held for a number of days to complete the autopsy and tests to try to discover some clues about who was responsible for the hit-and-run. The detectives from Sligo are looking around the area and have a good idea of the type of car involved. They first thought that it was someone from outside the area that was responsible, but for some reason, the Guards have changed their minds. They now believe that the car that hit poor Tom belongs to somebody from this parish. Don't ask me how they know that. The Guards are all over the place all morning, calling

58

to every bloody house in the parish looking for the car that hit Tom. They have drafted in Guards from all over the county. They must have discovered something, some new evidence," the publican said as he leaned over the bar and spoke in a whisper.

"I hope they get the bastard that killed him," Conor said. "He was a gentleman; he didn't deserve a death like that, alone on a cold, dark road like an animal."

After finishing off the pint, Conor went back home and decided to drive out to Darragh's house in Rossbeg to see how things were going. He took the route up Bridge Street and out the narrow Rossbeg road. As he drove out of town, he noticed several Garda squad cars at the part of the road where Tom Kearns was killed. Several Guards were standing looking into a ditch where a car had collided recently, probably the car involved in the hit-and-run. Conor drove on another few miles and noticed another squad car parked in a farmyard and three Guards walking around the farmyard and in and out of sheds.

After taking a few wrong turns and getting lost and asking directions, Conor eventually reached Darragh's house in Rossbeg. He parked his car at the front of the house next to Sarah's Mondeo.

There was a light on in the sitting room window. Conor reached behind him and grabbed a brown paper bag containing a bottle of Powers Whiskey that he had bought at O'Brien's for his visit. He got out of the car and walked towards the front door of the house, carefully picking his steps through the mud on the path leading to the front door. He knocked on the door and after a minute or so, the door opened.

"Hi, Conor, how are you?" Sarah asked as she opened the door.

"I'm grand, Sarah, and yourself?" Conor replied.

"Come in, come in," Sarah said as she opened the door fully and stood back to welcome Conor in. The kitchen was warm and cosy and smelt of burning turf.

"Sit down. Will you have a tea or a coffee?" Sarah asked.

"I'll take a mug of tea," Conor said as he sat down and took off his coat. Sarah went over to the kitchen area and rattled mugs about in the cupboard.

After chatting for a while on a range of meaningless topics, Conor asked, "Well, Sarah, how are you really getting on? Any word from Darragh?"

Sarah was quiet for a while and eventually said, "Oh, I don't know, I haven't seen Darragh since that last night. I only got back here yesterday myself, I got a lift back with Roisin. I stayed with her for a few days. When I got back, my car was outside. I came in and found a note on the table from Darragh, he wrote some shite that he was very sorry and that it will never happen again. He wrote that he was going to stay with his mother and sister in Sligo Town for a while to give me some time and space. He must have taken his car. It's gone from outside anyway. He told me it was fecked after running into a ditch a few nights before Christmas and it wouldn't start. He obviously got it going," Sarah said as she put turf into the stove.

"Well, do you think you will patch it up, Sarah, yourself and Darragh?" Conor asked.

"Ah, fuck him, Conor. I'm just fed up of it. It's going on for years. He is a good guy, but he just is unable to be faithful. I think I have taken him back too many times, I have given him too many chances. He just thinks he can walk all over me."

Sarah looked to the floor and then buried her face in her hands and burst into tears. Conor at first felt awkward and didn't know what to do. He got up from his armchair and went over to Sarah on the couch and put his arms around her to try to hold her and console her.

She cried on Conor's shoulder and then pulled back and said, "Oh, I'm sorry, Conor. You must feel caught in the middle, with Darragh being your best mate."

"It's okay. Here, have a shot of this stuff," Conor said as he got up to the table and brought over the bottle of whiskey and two small glasses from the kitchen and placed them on the coffee table on front of Sarah.

Sarah wiped her eyes with a hanky. She reached into her pockets, took out a pack of cigarettes, grabbed a box of matches from the coffee table and lit a fag. She pulled on the fag as Conor handed her a glass of whiskey.

"Thanks, Conor," she said as she sipped on the whiskey.

The pair chatted on for a few hours about craic at university in Galway. After nearly finishing half a bottle of whiskey between them, Sarah drifted off to sleep beside Conor on the couch. Conor let her sleep for a while and then, looking at the clock, realised it was almost two o'clock in the morning.

He went to shake Sarah on the shoulder, and as he did, her eyes opened slowly and she made eye contact. She reached out and, putting her arm around the back of his neck, pulled him towards her gently. Their lips came together and they kissed.

The kiss seemed to last for minutes, but probably, in reality, it was only a few seconds. Then suddenly Sarah pulled back and pushed Conor away. "Oh Christ, Conor, I'm so sorry. I didn't know what I was doing. I shouldn't have done that."

Conor turned his face away awkwardly. "It's okay, it's okay. Look, I best be off." He stood up.

"No, Conor, don't be daft. You can stay in the spare room. You are not in any fit state to drive home, especially not with all the Guards crawling around the area."

Conor went to walk towards the doorway and staggered slightly. "Yea, I suppose you're right," he said.

"Yea. Look, just take the bed in the spare room, the place where you stayed the other night," Sarah said as she directed Conor towards the spare room.

"Okay. I'll see you in the morning," Conor replied.

Conor felt unsure about how to react after what had happened. After opening the door into the spare room, he kicked off his boots, took off his jeans and shirt and got into bed. The room was cold and he shivered as he pulled the icy sheets up around him.

He found it hard to sleep with thoughts racing through his head. He drifted off for a while, then woke up and looked at his watch. It was 4.30. Something must have woken him.

He heard a knock on his bedroom door and as he was getting up out of bed to open it, the door opened. Sarah was standing in the hallway, which was half-lit by a stream of light from the kitchen. She walked into Conor's room, grabbed his hand and led him to her own room and into the double bed.

Chapter VIII

After All These Years

Saturday, 31st December 1988

The next morning, Conor woke up alongside Sarah to a loud thump at the front door. He looked over at the clock; it was 8.45 am.

"Who the fuck is that?" Sarah asked as she got up quickly and put on the dressing gown that was laid across a wicker chair beside the bed.

She walked out into the hall to peer through the net curtains to see who it was. "There's a bloody Garda squad car parked outside. What the feck do they want?"

A loud knock came at the door again. She came back into the bedroom and quickly put on the jeans that were on the window sill. Then she went to a chest of drawers and took out a pink t-shirt with 'The Pixies' written across it before putting on an old pair of runners. "You best stay here in bed, Conor. It might prevent some awkward questions."

"Okay, I suppose you're right," Conor replied watching Sarah walk into the kitchen to open the front door. In her hurry, she left the bedroom door half-open and he could hear her conversation with the Guards.

"Hello," Sarah said. "Can I help you? Is there something wrong?"

"Detective Jim Mulcahy, miss and this is Sergeant Sean Burns. We are just carrying out searches on all properties in the area in relation to a recent hit-and-run incident. Do you mind if we come in and ask you a few questions?"

"Sure, come on in. I'm sorry it took me a while to answer the door—I was in bed."

"It's okay, miss. I'm very sorry that we got you up; we realise that it is the Christmas holidays. Do you mind if I smoke, by the way?"

"No, no problem. I'll get you an ashtray. Sorry it's so cold in here—I didn't get around to lighting up the stove yet," Sarah said. "Will you have tea or coffee?"

"A coffee for me please," said Detective Mulcahy.

"I'm grand," said Sergeant Burns. "I'll take nothing, thanks."

"Well, are you any nearer to finding the scumbag that killed Tom Kearns?" Sarah asked.

"No, unfortunately not. We are still ... looking into a few, er, things. Now, miss, I apologise for calling at such an early hour. It is 'miss', isn't it? Or is it 'Mrs'?" Jim Mulcahy asked.

"It's miss."

"This is just routine, miss. We have to call to every house in the area. I hope you understand. Your name, please, miss?"

"Sarah Gallagher."

"You're not from around here, Sarah. That's not a Sligo accent."

"No, I'm from Letterkenny, in Donegal."

"Do you work local?"

"Yea, I work in the Bank of Ireland in Ballygalvin."

"Do you have a car, Sarah?" Detective Mulcahy asked.

"Yea, the Ford Mondeo parked outside."

"The other car outside—the Opel—who owns that car?"

"A friend of mine who stayed over last night."

"Can I ask who it is?"

"Just a friend. His name is Conor Doyle. Well, actually, he is more of a friend of my boyfriend. He just called up to see him last night and my boyfriend wasn't here. He said he would wait 'til he got back. It got late and he stayed over in the spare room."

"You said you have a boyfriend," Detective Mulcahy said. "Does he live here?"

"Yea … but he went over to see his mother in Sligo Town. I expected him back last night, but he must have met up with friends. You know how it is at Christmas time. He probably will be home sometime later today. Will you have another cup of coffee?" Sarah asked.

"No, we're fine." Detective Mulcahy responded. "What's your boyfriend's name, Sarah?"

"He is Darragh Lonigan."

"Is he anything to do with the former county councillor, James Lonigan, who lived in this area?"

"Yea, a son of his," Sarah replied.

"Really? I used to know his father, James, very well. He was a good man, a great man to get things done, a good man for Ballinastrad. So that makes Darragh a nephew of Eamonn Lonigan, the T.D. in Galway. Now there is a man who is very influential," Jim Mulcahy said.

"Oh, I think I know your boyfriend, Sarah. He frequents the bars in Ballinastrad quite a bit," Sergeant Burns said.

"Yea, you could find him in Sheehan's regularly, all right," Sarah replied.

"You said he has gone to Sligo, Sarah, to see his mother. Does he have a car?"

"Yes, an old Toyota Starlet. I'm surprised he brought it to Sligo. It was giving him a bit of trouble."

"What kind of trouble?"

"Oh, it's the alternator. I think it's faulty or something. I'm sorry, I know damn all about cars. He said it was hard starting at times. He tells me things about the car, and I don't really listen, I just remember him saying something about a faulty alternator."

"How old is your boyfriend's car?"

"It's about eight years old, I think."

"Okay, do you know the registration number and the colour?" Jim Mulcahy asked.

"Oh, it's a kind of a pale sky blue, with plenty of rust on it. I'm sorry, I don't know the registration. Hold on, I might have it on something. Give me a minute to look for it," Sarah replied.

"Take your time, Sarah."

Conor could hear Sarah opening and closing drawers and cupboards in the kitchen for a few minutes.

"Here, take this, detective. It's a car tax form that has the registration number of Darragh's car on it," Sarah said.

"Thanks, Sarah. When did you say your boyfriend was due back again?" Jim asked.

"Sometime today, maybe tomorrow. When Darragh meets his mates in Sligo, it can take a while."

"Yes, I understand. Well, that's fine, Miss Gallagher. Look, we might take a look around outside and we will call back in a day or two when Darragh gets back, just to ask him a few routine questions. I hope you don't mind?"

"Sure, that's okay."

"Oh and thank you for the coffee, Miss Gallagher."

"No problem. Good luck with your enquiries and I hope you get whoever is responsible for killing Tom soon. I believe his funeral is on later this morning," Sarah said.

"It is. That's why we are doing our enquiries so early. Thank you again, Miss Gallagher and Happy New Year," Detective Mulcahy said.

"Oh yea, it's New Year's Eve. I almost forgot. Well, goodbye."

Conor could hear the front door closing and Sarah walking back down to the bedroom.

"Well, they are gone, thank God," Sarah said.

"Yea, I could hear all the chat from the room here," Conor replied.

"It was just a routine visit, they said. They are calling on everybody. They asked a few questions about Darragh and where he was. It was a bit awkward. They wanted to know where his car was," Sarah said as she sat on the side of the bed and watched Conor get dressed.

"Don't worry about it, Sarah, they are asking everybody questions. I suppose they have to."

"Yea, I suppose you're right."

Conor sat down on the bed beside Sarah and put his arm around her and hugged her.

"Look, I better be heading off. I have to go to the funeral. Me auld fella will be going mad with no car," Conor said.

"Do you want some breakfast?" Sarah asked.

"I'll take a quick cup of tea," Conor said, walking out towards the kitchen.

After finishing his tea, Conor got up from the table and put on his coat. "Look, I'll be off. Will I see you later this evenin?"

"Yea, I might meet you for a drink later. I'll see you about eight in Sheehan's," Sarah replied.

"That's grand," Conor said as he gave Sarah a kiss on the cheek and went out the front door.

It was just starting to snow; light flakes were floating gently down to the cold ground. Conor rubbed his hands as he got into the car. He started it up and headed back home. The sky was getting dark as the snow was getting heavier.

After having a quick shower, Conor walked up with his parents to the church for the funeral for Tom Kearns.

The funeral service was due to start at eleven. It was now 10.30 and the church was nearly full, apart from the reserved seats at the front. Conor and his parents took a seat at the back of the church. Tom was a well-known and well-liked man. He never missed a local funeral or removal himself.

The bell rang outside the church and a few minutes later, the church door opened to a cold breeze as Tom's coffin was shouldered in by four middle-aged men and a younger man in his twenties. Conor's father told him that it was Tom's two brothers from America and his brother-in-law and nephew. Regina, Tom's daughter and her two sons followed. Regina wiped her eyes as she walked and held on tightly to her son's arms. A tall, bald man walked behind her, presumably her husband. Father Gerry Mulvey walked at the front of the procession, turning around to bless the coffin.

During the service, Father Mulvey spoke about how Tom had found solace in the church after the death of his wife Maureen many years ago and how Tom always attended Mass every Sunday and was always available to do any jobs that needed doing around the church and local national school. Tom was always reliable and always had time to help anybody in need. Father Mulvey also urged anybody who had any information about the hit-and-run incident to come forward to the relevant authorities.

After sympathising with Tom's daughter and brothers, Conor and his parents stood beside the grave to watch Tom's remains being lowered into the cold, dark earth. Snow was falling on the coffin as it slowly descended. Regina's tears and cries were blended with a song that was sung by a young teenage girl with red hair. She sung one of Tom's favourite songs, *'After All These Years'*, which had been made famous by the ballad group Foster and Allen.

Conor wasn't a lover of sentimental, middle-of-the-road ballads of the country and Irish genre and would often poke fun at the first note of them when they came on the radio. However, he felt emotional whilst listening to the red-headed teenage girl singing accompanied by a spotty, lanky, dark-haired lad on acoustic guitar. Conor looked over at the snow falling on the black coat that Tom's daughter, Regina, wrapped around herself as she tossed a white rose into the grave onto her father's coffin. The sombre scene got to him and he could see eyes going watery and red on many grown men standing beside him.

As Conor left the graveyard, he stopped to talk to old school pals. The talk centred around the tragedy of Tom's death. One of the lads in the group mentioned that his cousin was a Guard and was involved in the investigation, and that he had heard that the Guards had found a burnt-out car the evening before that they thought could belong to the person responsible for the hit-and-run.

The car was supposedly discovered in a laneway headed to an old disused quarry about twenty miles away, near to Glengarrif. They assumed that perhaps the owner was attempting to push the car into the flooded quarry hole, but the car got stuck on the muddy pass. The muddy lane was ploughed up and it looked like, after failing to get the car unstuck, the owner had panicked and torched it. The number plates were removed and no documentation belonging to the owner was found, but the Guards were looking for a VIN or chassis number or something. If they find one, they might be able to trace it back to the owner.

The conversation then changed to the more pressing issue of where to go later, as it was New Year's Eve. Conor arranged to meet them for a pint or two in town.

He headed back down to his home and had dinner with his parents.

"I forgot to tell you, Conor, that there was a phone call for you here last night about nine o'clock from your friend Darragh," Conor's mother said.

"Oh yea? What did he say? Did he leave a message?"

"He just asked where you were. I told him that you had gone out to meet a friend. I think he said that he was ringing from Galway. It was hard to make out what he was saying, he sounded drunk. I think he said that he would ring back at six this evening."

"Okay, thanks for letting me know, anyway, Mum. I feel a bit knackered. I might go upstairs and lie down for a while," Conor said as he yawned.

After lazing around in his bedroom listening to his old records and reading a book all afternoon, Conor went down to the sitting room to wait for Darragh's phone call. He felt nervous at the thought of talking to him after what had happened the night before with Sarah. He thought about telling him the truth. How would Darragh react? Would he be upset or angry, or would he not give a fuck?

Conor looked at the clock on the mantelpiece; it was five minutes to six. He stared at the clock and then down to the open fire below. The sticks were crackling and sparking. The fireguard was sitting in front of the fire to protect the 'good' carpet, which was well-worn at this stage. The Labrador was stretched out on the mat in front of the warm fire. The dog wagged his tail hard against the floor as Conor looked over at him.

Conor looked to the clock again. It was only just gone six o'clock. Darragh would hardly ring on time anyway.

He might not ring at all. He was probably pissed in a pub somewhere and wouldn't even remember. *Just as well*, Conor thought, as he wanted to avoid talking to him at this point.

Twenty minutes passed and still no phone call. Conor went over to the window of the sitting room to have a look at what was happening outside on Main Street. The snow

71

was continuing to fall. There was a heavy white coat of snow on the road outside and the cars coming along the road were driving slowly and carefully. Kids were grabbing huge handfuls of snow off parked cars and pelting each other.

It didn't seem that long ago that Conor and Darragh were at the same craic. They'd loved the snowy days. Especially when they'd gotten days off school.

Conor went back to the chair beside the fire. He looked at the photos on the mantelpiece. There were several black and white photographs: one of his parents on their wedding day back in 1953, another of Conor and his older brother Sean when they were at primary school back in the late sixties.

Sean had lived in Dublin for the last eight years. There was a large colour picture of Sean and his wife and their two young daughters up on the mantelpiece in a gold-coloured frame.

Conor was falling into a half-sleep looking into the fire when the phone rang. He rushed over nervously to pick up the phone.

"Hello, hello, hello." There was a short silence.

"Is that the Doyles in Ballinastrad? I'm not too sure if I have the right number," said the female voice.

It took a while for Conor to register who it was.

"Is that Sarah?" he asked.

"Yea, it is," Sarah replied. "Hi, Conor, how are you? I wasn't sure if I was through to the right number. I had to look for your parent's number in the phone book."

"Where are you ringing from?" Conor asked. He knew that there was no phone in Darragh and Sarah's house.

"I'm ringing from Greegan's post office in Rossbeg, I just drove down here from the house. It took me ages to get here. The roads are desperate with the snow. Look, I'm just ringing to tell you that I won't be coming down tonight for a drink, in case you were waiting for me at the bar. I'm sorry, the roads are just cat. I was sliding around the place getting down here to the post office; I don't want to chance driving into Ballinastrad. I would never get up some of those bloody hills on the way in. I hope you don't mind," Sarah said.

"No, no, it's fine. Christ, don't be daft driving down. I didn't realise the roads are so bad. It's probably worse up at the mountains where you are," Conor replied.

"Yea, it's as bad as I have seen them up here. It's been snowing heavy since you left this morning," Sarah said "I'm looking out the window at the snow falling on my car."

"Look, I hope you make it back to your house all right. You will have a quiet time on your own for New Year's Eve. I suppose I wouldn't make it out to you either," Conor replied.

"No, you wouldn't have a hope. Look, I'll be fine. I'll watch some crap TV. Call up tomorrow if the roads are clear," Sarah said.

"I will," Conor said.

"Look, I better go, Conor. The snow isn't easing off. Happy New Year."

"Happy New Year, Sarah. Bye. See you tomorrow."

Conor thought for a moment after the phone call. All kinds of ideas were going through his head. Were the bad snowy roads just an excuse? Did Sarah regret what had happened the night before? Did she want to avoid seeing him? But why then would she invite him up tomorrow?

As all the thoughts were spiralling around, the phone rang again. Conor picked it up.

"Hi, Conor, it's Darragh."

"Hi. How's the craic? Where are you?" Conor asked.

"I'm in Galway City, back in our old stomping ground, Conor. I just fancied a change of scenery until things blow over, until Sarah calms down. I thought I would give her some breathing space. Sure, you know the craic yourself."

"Yea. How long are you staying over there?" Conor asked.

"I don't really know—maybe a few more days. That's why I'm ringing you, Conor. Come on over. It will be a laugh. Come over tomorrow—a few pints on New Year's Day in Galway city. What could be better?"

Conor hesitated. He thought about what Sarah had said about calling over tomorrow. But did she really want him to call over? He was unsure.

"Yea, Darragh, okay. I'll meet you so in Galway. Whereabouts?"

"In the Quays Pub at five o'clock. That will give you time to get over," Darragh said.

"Okay, Darragh, I'll see you there, so. I wouldn't mind a change of scenery from Ballinastrad myself, to be honest."

"Good man. I'll see you tomorrow. Happy New Year, Conor," Darragh roared down the phone.

"Happy New Year to you too, Darragh, you mad bastard. Good luck."

Conor was unsure if he had made the right choice in agreeing to go to Galway the next day.

Then he decided it was for the best. He needed a break from Ballinastrad and he thought that Darragh and Sarah would eventually patch things up in a week or so. The night that he shared with Sarah was probably a stupid mistake, and she probably regretted it now, so it was best to just forget it ever happened and say nothing to Darragh about it. It was just a drunken mistake, he kept telling himself.

He rang up the bus timetable information and was told that there was a bus leaving Glengarrif for Galway at 1.30 tomorrow afternoon. Rather than going out, he decided to prepare himself for probably a day or two marathon drinking binges with Darragh in Galway. He spent New Year's Eve at home with his parents and had a few drinks in the house before going to bed around one in the morning.

Chapter IX

New Year's Day

Sunday, 1st January 1989

Conor's eyes opened. He stared over at the clock on the bedside locker. It was quarter past eight, and just getting bright outside. A faint beam of sunlight pierced through the opening in the blue curtains.

He turned away from the light and thought about catching another few hours' sleep. His bus was not until 1.30 and he would probably get very little sleep over the next night or two in Galway. As much as he tried though, he couldn't drift off to sleep again.

He had nearly forgotten that it was New Year's Day, the start of a new morning, a new day, a new month and a new year. It was 1989, the last year of the eighties. 1988 was gone now.

It wasn't a bad year, he thought. He was established now in London with a reasonably good job and a nice apartment. He had some good mates in London. The highlight of the year was when Ray Houghton had scored the winning goal against England in Stuggart in June. The cheers had been deafening in all the Irish bars in Kilburn. They had got one over on England the old enemy.

Most English people treated the Irish well over in London. They were friendly and helpful.

But there was an underlying tension. The struggle in the north of Ireland between the IRA and the British forces had frequently spilt over to the British mainland. This made life difficult. Occasionally, skinhead yobs would shout abuse at Conor and his Irish mates as they came out of Irish bars, things like "Fuck off back home, Paddy" or "You murdering Irish bastards". They just ignored it. Conor had heard stories of Irish lads being kicked to death if they responded to the taunts from the skinheads. It was best to keep your head down.

What would the New Year bring? Conor wondered as he lay in bed.

Unable to drift back to sleep, he decided to get up. After having a shower, he packed a small bag that he found in the bottom of his wardrobe. He went downstairs and made himself tea and toast. His mother had his dinner ready for him early at 12.30. She knew he wouldn't be eating too well once he got to Galway.

Afterwards, Conor's dad drove him the twelve miles to Rathalgin to get the Sligo bus to Galway. As he got out of the car, Conor told his father that he would probably be back in a day or two.

He waited at the bus stop and pulled up his heavy black coat around his neck as the cold January wind bit hard. The early morning rain had washed away much of the snow that had fallen during the previous day and night, but some patches still clung to the fields around Rathalgin.

The half-one bus arrived at quarter to two. Conor paid seven pounds to a grumpy-looking bus driver and took a seat. The bus and driver chugged along half-asleep. The drone of the engine was only intermittently drowned out by a heavy grinding of the gear box.

The bus was almost empty. There were only six other passengers on board. An elderly couple sat in the seat in front of Conor. Down the back, three lads in their early twenties were slouched across the long backseat. They looked the worse for wear, probably suffering the after-effects of New Year's Eve. One of them sucked on a fag, and the smoke drifted around the seats at the rear of the bus.

At the front of the bus sat a girl with long black hair that stretched over the shoulders of a long, brown suede coat. She was reading a book. Maybe she was catching up on some study for her course work. She looked the student type, hippy and bohemian, like the many that gathered around Galway City. She reminded him of Sarah.

Sarah had been the cool, good-looking girl in first Arts in UCG back in 1981. She'd looked like a clone of Chrissie Hynde from the rock group The Pretenders back then. She'd had jet black hair and wore heavy, dark eyeliner. She'd copied Chrissie Hynde's look with a short black leather jacket, a tight black t-shirt and figure-hugging jeans. She'd truly been a Chrissie Hynde pretender, but younger and better-looking.

Before Conor and Darragh had gotten to know her, they'd watched her strutting into the English lectures. They would discuss her attributes as they sat at the back of the lecture hall. They'd even gotten up early to actually attend ten o'clock lectures so they might get a chance to chat to her.

It had been Conor that got chatting to her first. They got talking one night in a bar when Conor and Darragh were on one of their marathon piss-ups. Darragh had been out of his tree, so it had been left to Conor to make the introductions.

They'd hit it off straight away. They'd had a similar taste in music and she had a great dry sense of humour that complimented Conor's. They'd met for coffee in the students' union afterwards and had begun to hang out together at English and Philosophy lectures. Conor had been smitten by her the first time he met her, but somehow it had just stayed as a friendship between them for months.

One night at a party after a few too many beers, Sarah and Conor had gotten it together. They'd both felt awkward afterwards, yet it had tended to happen every few weeks on a casual basis. It had been clear that Conor was very interested in her, but he hadn't been sure if she'd felt the same way.

A few months later, events had taken a bit of a twist. It was at a disco at CJ's in November of 1981 that Darragh had begun to edge in on Sarah. Eventually, after a few nights on the beer around the city, Darragh had brought Sarah back to the apartment that he shared with Conor. Darragh, who had rarely slept alone during his student days, had confessed to Conor one night that he was at last in love and had found his soul mate.

Conor hadn't passed much remarks on this until Darragh had informed him that his soul mate was Sarah. Conor had been shocked and annoyed, but had never let Darragh become aware of this, and he'd sat back as he watched Sarah spend more and more time with Darragh. From there on, Darragh and Sarah had begun going out.

Conor had been jealous at first. But after a time, he'd learned to accept it, or at least, he'd pretend to as the days, weeks, months and years passed by in college. He hadn't wanted to fall out with Darragh or Sarah.

The trio had become inseparable in Galway during their three years there. Conor had plenty of girlfriends there too, but no relationships that lasted more than a few weeks or months at the most.

Conor's thoughts drifted forward to recent events, the phone call he had received from Sarah the previous night and how she couldn't come down to Ballinastrad because of the snowy roads. Was it just an excuse to avoid an awkward situation meeting him? Did she regret what had happened the night before? Should he tell Darragh about what had happened? How would he react?

Conor tried not to think about it, choosing to instead look forward to a good night out in Galway. He wanted to visit the old haunts that Darragh and himself used to frequent. He wanted to see what had changed.

The bus pulled to a stop at Ceannt Station beside Eyre Square in Galway City Centre at around four o'clock. It was a bright, cold and frosty evening.

Eyre Square looked quiet. There were very few people around. The day after the night before, New Year's Day was usually a day for relaxing at home and nursing a severe hangover.

Conor got off the bus and threw his small luggage bag across his shoulder. He headed down William Street and onto Shop Street towards the Quays Bar to meet Darragh.

Back in their student days, Conor and Darragh hadn't really drunk around the city centre that much. They'd mainly gone on the piss around Salthill, drinking in the Castle, the Warwick and CJ's.

Conor looked at his watch as he entered the front door of the Quays Bar. It was 4.15; he was meant to meet Darragh in the bar at five.

It was quiet and dark inside. There were plenty of vacant bar stools. He grabbed one and sat on it, placing his bag on another next to him. An older man in a grey jacket was sitting further down the bar, pulling at the end of a fag. A group of lads were standing around the pool table. After a few minutes, a bar man appeared coming up from the steps of the cellar beneath the bar.

"Well, sorry to keep you. Had to change a barrel. What will you have?" he asked Conor.

"A pint of stout, please," Conor replied.

After the pint had settled, the bearded bar man passed Conor over his pint. Conor paid him and sat quietly as he sipped at what would be the first of many, he thought.

There was a battle going on in the bar between a musical on the telly—which looked like Yule Brynner's cue ball head in *'The King and I'*—and the jukebox that was blasting out *'Jailbreak'* by Thin Lizzy. The jukebox was winning the battle.

Conor remembered going along with Darragh and Sarah to see Thin Lizzy play at the Leisureland in Salthill in 1983. It had been a brilliant gig, Lizzy's farewell 'Thunder and Lightning' tour. He would have loved to have seen them during their peak in the late seventies with Brian Robertson or Gary Moore.

He drank two more pints and there was still no sign of Darragh. It was almost six o'clock. He knew that Darragh was never a great timekeeper. What if he'd forgotten? What if he was pissed and asleep in some bar?

Maybe he had hooked up with a woman in some apartment. Maybe he had rung Sarah and she had told him all about what had happened, that she and Conor had slept together. Where the fuck would he sleep tonight if Darragh didn't turn up? He thought about maybe arranging some accommodation before it got too late.

At about seven o'clock, Conor was just finishing off a fourth pint and had gotten directions from the bar man for a bed and breakfast up the street. He walked out the front door and turned right.

Then he heard a familiar roar behind him. "Hey Doyle, you bastard, where da fuck are you goin'?" It was Darragh. "Where you goin', Conor? I thought we were meeting for a pint at five in the Quays." He gave Conor a bear hug.

Conor smiled. "It's fucking after seven, you drunken asshole."

"Is it?" Darragh looked at his watch. "Oh yea, you're right. Sorry about that. I got held up in a pub down the street. I got chatting to a nice blonde babe about Charles Bukowski and other shit. Unfortunately, her husband turned up and that ended that." He laughed. "So what's the plan, Conor?"

Conor looked at Darragh. He was well pissed. "Have you eaten anything, Darragh?"

"No, feck that. Eatin' is cheatin'," Darragh replied.

"Come on, we will grab some fish and chips across the road. I'm a bit hungry myself," Conor said.

After the two mates finished their fine meal of cod and chips standing outside Luigi's chipper, they headed to an old haunt of theirs called the Harbour Bar and took a table in the corner. Conor thought it best to keep Darragh off the high stools in case he fell over.

Conor ordered two pints of stout and a Powers Whiskey for himself. He thought he would have to try to catch up with Darragh to get on the same wavelength.

"Well, any craic at home?" Darragh asked Conor.

"No, not really. I was just at Tom Kearns's funeral yesterday. It was huge. The church was packed. They still haven't found the bastard that killed poor Tom. The cops are searching all the houses in the area. They thought it was somebody from Sligo who was responsible. Now they think it was somebody local. They found a burnt-out car yesterday. They think that it could be the car involved in the hit-and-run," Conor replied.

"I hope they get the guy responsible," Darragh said, and he got up to go to the toilet.

Two hours passed quickly as the two old friends laughed and joked. Darragh had got a new lease on life and appeared to be more sober now than when Conor met him at seven. Or maybe that was Conor getting fairly merry himself.

The pretty bar maid had a good taste in music and was playing a cassette mix tape of some great rock songs. The intro to The Doors' song *'Riders on the Storm'* came on, and Darragh got up and did his best Jim Morrison impression in the middle of the flagstone floor.

The dance came to a sudden end when he swayed backwards and fell over a table and stools next to him. Conor staggered over to pick him up and the pair of them just roared laughing. The bar was nearly empty and nobody seemed to even notice. The bar maid just said, "Take it easy, lads," as she smiled over while polishing a whiskey glass.

The next track on was *'Brass in Pocket'* by The Pretenders. Conor and Darragh smiled and immediately thought of Sarah.

Darragh's face slowly turned from a smile to a look of depression. "I fucked up, Conor. I really fucked up this time."

Conor tried to console Darragh even though deep down he didn't think that Sarah would take him back this time. He had gone too far and had tried his luck too many times before. This made Conor think that perhaps himself and Sarah might have a future now, but how would he tell that to Darragh?

Uncertain at this point how to approach this predicament, Conor took the easy way out for now. "Look, give it time; it's only been a few days. She will get over it. She will give you another chance."

"No, not this time. I think that's it. Maybe it's time to move on. I have been thinking about moving back here to Galway. I'm sick and tired of fuckin' Ballinastrad anyway. It's starting to bore the ass off me. There's a good scene here for painting. Maybe I'll move to Connemara or the Aran islands and become a fisherman."

Darragh laughed as he burst into a line of *'Fisherman's Blues'* by The Waterboys. Conor noticed that Darragh was acting strangely; his emotions were erratic, up and down like a seesaw.

A few minutes later, Darragh's mood changed again, and he stared at the floor.

Conor felt sorry for him. He felt guilty about what had happened between himself and Sarah. He was on the verge of telling him about it. "Look, man, don't feel so bad. There is something I need to let you know."

Darragh lifted his head and looked over at Conor. "What are you going to tell me Conor? Is it that you're … gay?"

"Fuck off, ya stupid prick," Conor said and the two of them roared laughing as Darragh hit Conor a friendly jab to the shoulder that nearly knocked him off his stool.

"Come on," Darragh said. "Let's go someplace else. This place is a bit dead."

The drunken duo staggered out into the Galway night towards a nearby bar called Morgan's, where they could hear a live band playing. They drank away and listened to the rock band until closing time at 11.30.

"Well, where we are going to stay tonight? I'm feeling wrecked," Conor said.

"I booked you a room in a hotel I have been staying in for the last few nights. It's a shithole, but it's cheap," Darragh said.

"Grand, any place will do, Conor replied. "Well, lead the way, my good man."

Darragh ploughed the ten minute walk towards the Waterfront Hotel followed by Conor as he staggered behind. They collected their keys at the front desk, noticed that the residents' bar was open and decided to go in for a few more beverages.

As Darragh drank more and more shots of Powers, Conor noticed that he was saying less and less. Not the usual Darragh, who had a titanic capacity for drink and often went forty-eight hours on the tear with very little sleep.

"How long were you out drinking before I met you?" Conor asked, trying to resurrect a conversation. "Are you boozing all day?"

"No, I didn't start until one o'clock," Darragh said quietly.

There was silence again.

"Are you okay, Darragh?" Conor asked.

There was little response.

"Christ, I don't know what to do. I really fucked up," Darragh said, placing his head in his hands.

Conor thought about telling his friend about his night with Sarah to make him feel less guilty. He thought that then perhaps Darragh would be angry with him, but he wouldn't feel so low if he discovered that Sarah had technically two-timed him as well.

"Fuck, the poor bastard," Darragh said.

"What are you taking about, Darragh? Who are you talking about?"

"Tom, dying like an animal on the cold, dark road, alone. He didn't deserve that. Nobody deserves that, nobody deserves to die like that." Darragh was mumbling and very incoherent.

"What you are muttering about?" Conor asked.

This time, Darragh raised his voice and roared, "Fuckin' Tom Kearns."

The three men drinking at the bar turned their heads. The night porter who was pulling a pint gave Darragh a dirty look.

"Yea, Darragh, it's terrible. I hope they get the scum bag that killed him," Conor said.

"Yea …" Darragh said. "Yea … oh Christ, Conor." He placed his head in his hands again and began muttering to himself once more. Conor could hear his mutterings turn to sobs as tears ran down his face. "Conor, Conor. What will I do?"

"What do you mean?" Conor asked.

There was silence for a minute. Then, with his face still in his hands, facing away from Conor, Darragh said slowly and clearly, "It was me, Conor. I killed him. I killed Tom."

Conor didn't know what to say. He was in a state of shock and confusion. Was this a sick joke, or was Darragh just raving with too much whiskey?

After what seemed like a long time but was only probably only a half a minute, Conor asked Darragh, "Are you serious or taking the piss, because it's a sick fuckin joke?"

Darragh turned towards Conor. "I am deadly serious, Conor. I can't keep it in anymore." Tears still dripped down from his red eyes.

"I hit him. I wasn't sure if he was alive or dead. I just drove on. I left him there to die like a dog. I was drinking all day that day in Sheehan's. I drove out the Rossbeg road. I was steamed. I couldn't see out through the windscreen; it was covered in frost. I hit an icy patch on the road. The car slid in towards the ditch. I tried to steer away from it. The car rammed off a tree or something, then swerved out and I heard a wallop. I didn't know what it was. I stopped the car and got out."

"It was so dark. At first I didn't know what I had hit. I thought it was a deer or something. Then I looked down and heard a man groaning. It was Tom. There was blood running down his face. His legs were all twisted. I just panicked. I got back into the car and drove off. I could have saved him; he was still alive. I just drove off home. I told nobody. I kept it hidden inside me all this time. But it's eating me up. I kept a big front up, a facade. Darragh, the loud joker, acted the fool, the clown, as usual, so I hoped no one would suspect anything. I kept drinking heavy, but then, I was always bloody drinking heavy. I'm a bloody sham, a fake, a waster. A fuckin' selfish fuckin' murderer."

"What are you going to do, Darragh?" Conor asked. "Are you going to tell the cops?"

"I don't know, Conor. I suppose I should."

"Is that your car that they found burnt-out beside the quarry hole beside Glengarrif?" Conor asked.

"Yea, it is," Darragh replied.

"Look, in a few days the cops will trace it to you. Maybe you should tell them. You might get off a bit lighter."

"Yea, maybe," Darragh said. He seemed to calm himself as if it was a relief to finally tell somebody. "Christ, this been eating me up for the last ten days."

Conor was devastated by Darragh's confession. He felt sorry for him. He knew once he informed the Guards, his life would be on a different path. He would face ridicule, bitterness, anger and a long prison sentence. He would lose his close friends.

He also felt anger towards Darragh for what he had done, killing a harmless man on the road. He was disappointed that Darragh's life would be changed forever. He was also disappointed that his closest and oldest friend was such a coward for not stopping to try to see if he could have possibly saved Tom Kearns's life. If he could have driven to a nearby house to ring for an ambulance, maybe Tom might have survived.

"Will you come with me to the Garda station in the morning, Conor?"

"I will, Darragh," Conor replied. He looked at the clock over the bar. "We better get some sleep. It's almost four o'clock."

The two old friends walked silently out of the bar and up the stairs to their rooms. Conor was in 127 and Darragh next door in 128.

"I'll give you a rap on the door at around ten in the morning," Conor said.

"Grand," Darragh replied. He smiled over at Conor with the big grin he had often greeted him with since the days they were in primary school together. However, this time, Conor thought it was more of a goodbye than a greeting, because once they went to the Garda station in the morning, that was it. Their lives would be on very different roads.

Chapter X

A Pagan Place

Monday, 2nd January 1989

Despite the fact that Conor had so much to drink the day and night before, he couldn't really sleep, as too many thoughts about Darragh were criss-crossing in his mind. He only drifted off at about 6.30 and what only seemed like five minutes later, he was awoken by the sound of a lorry chugging outside and the clanging of empty beer barrels that rang like bells.

He sat up in the bed and squinted at his watch. It was 11.15. He got out of bed and pulled on the clothes that he had worn the night before, which were strewn across the floor. His paisley shirt stank of cigarette smoke. He went into the bathroom and brushed his teeth to wash away the stale taste of alcohol.

He didn't feel too bad, only a slight headache. Maybe the hangover hadn't kicked in yet. Probably he was so caught up in the revelation from the night before that he was in shock and his system was running on adrenalin.

He grabbed his bag and closed the bedroom door behind him. He knocked on Darragh's room door in the dark hotel hallway. There was no reply. He knocked several times, but no reply.

He went downstairs to the lobby and asked if the receptionist could ring Darragh's room, 128. The lady receptionist was about to ring when she asked, "Did you say room 128? Oh, sorry. He's already checked out."

"Are you sure?" Conor asked, scratching his head. "When did he check out?"

The receptionist checked the large register in front of her. "He checked out about two hours ago, at 9.30."

"Did he leave a message?" Conor asked.

"No, sorry sir. No message."

Conor paid his bill at the desk. He wondered where Darragh had gone to.

Had he gone to a local Garda station himself? Maybe his conscience hadn't allowed him to wait for his friend to get up and accompany him.

Conor was unsure what to do now. Should he go and look for Darragh? But he didn't know which Garda station to enquire to. Maybe he hadn't gone to a Garda station at all. Maybe he'd gone back to Ballinastrad. Maybe he had gone on the run to God knew where.

After having a mug of coffee in the front bar of the hotel, Conor decided to take a walk around nearby streets just in case he might stumble across Darragh. He walked in and out of bars to check if he had gone back on the beer.

The futile search continued for two hours. Freezing, sleety rain was falling. It was pointless just walking about.

Conor decided to check back in the hotel they had stayed in the night before.

"Hi, I think I was talking to you a few hours ago," he said to the receptionist. "My name is Conor Doyle. I stayed here last night in room 127. I asked you earlier about my friend Darragh Lonigan, who stayed in room 128. You told me that he checked out early this morning. The problem is that I can't find him anywhere and I was just wondering if he'd called back here and left a message for me."

"Okay, sir. Well, I have been here most of the morning and I received no message from your friend. What was his name again, sir?" the girl at the reception desk asked.

"Darragh Lonigan, a tall guy with longish red hair. Scruffy-looking."

"I don't remember getting any message, sir. I will just ask some of the other staff members. I will be back in a minute." The receptionist walked into the office behind the desk and returned a few minutes later. "No, sorry sir. No message from a Darragh Lonigan. I'm sorry I can't help you. I hope you find him."

"That's okay, thanks. Bye."

Conor decided that he might as well head back to Ballinastrad. He rang the bus station from the hotel to check the time for the next bus home. There was one leaving in fifteen minutes from Ceannt Station at Eyre Square. He then rang home to tell his parents that he was getting the three o'clock bus and that he should be in Rathalgin at around five. His dad said that he would pick him up there. He asked if Darragh had rung the house and his father replied that he hadn't.

After legging it up Shop Street and William Street and down through a busy and wet Eyre Square, Conor made his bus just as it was about to pull out of the bus station. He had a good choice of seats because the bus was only half full.

The three o'clock news was on the bus radio. He tried to listen to see if there was any mention of developments in the Kearns' hit-and-run case, but there was no mention of it.

About an hour into the journey, there was nobody left on the bus but Conor. The bus stopped in a small village outside a building that appeared to be a grocer's shop, a post office and a pub. The bus driver got off the bus and went in.

After about ten minutes, the driver still hadn't come back. Conor assumed that he was picking up or dropping off a parcel in the post office.

He was eager to get home to find out what had happened to Darragh. He was also busting for a leak, so he decided to get off the bus himself and go into the toilets in the small country pub. As he pushed in the front door, he discovered the bus driver sitting up at the small counter talking to an old woman behind the bar. He was sinking a creamy pint of stout and had another full one in front of him.

"Well, how's things now, young fella? Did you get fed up waiting on the bus? We will be heading off in five minutes. Will you have a pint?" the bus driver asked Conor.

"No, you're fine, thanks," Conor replied.

"Are you sure?" asked the driver as he sank the end of his first pint.

"Ah, I'll have a quick half one of Powers, so. Thanks."

Conor went off to the toilet and came back and knocked back his whiskey as the driver swallowed his second pint in two big mouthfuls. The man then gave a loud burp and said to the old lady behind the bar, "thanks Rosemary, that was mighty, the best pint in the county of Galway."

He placed his driver's hat on his head, got up off his stool, walked outside into the darkening evening and got back on the bus. Conor followed him out and onto the bus, then decided that he looked daft sitting at the back of the bus on his own and moved up towards the front to chat to the driver. The pair chatted on the way to Rathalgin about football and the best pubs in Galway and Sligo for good drink and loose women.

Conor introduced himself and told the driver that he was from Ballinastrad. The driver did likewise: his name was Ollie Fitzpatrick from Ballygalvin originally, but he'd been living in Sligo Town for the last thirty years.

When Ollie found out where Conor was from, he was full of questions about the residents of the town and surrounding area. He seemed to know everyone, who they were married to and who their fathers were. He knew more about the people of Ballinastrad than Conor did.

"It was terrible about Tom Kearns," Conor said, thinking that Ollie was bound to have heard about it.

"Yea and the Guards are no further on now finding out who killed him," Ollie replied.

"I heard that they found a burnt-out car that they believe belonged to the person responsible for the hit-and-run. And that it wouldn't be too long 'til they traced it to the owner," Conor said as he offered Ollie a fag, which he accepted.

"Naw, that was a dead end. It came to nothing. The car was in bits; it had exploded. They couldn't find any evidence on it. The number plates had been removed and they couldn't make out any chassis numbers or anything.

Sure, that car might not be anything to do with the incident. It could just have been a stolen car, burned out by young lads, joy riders or whatever the feck you call them. I tell you, the Guards are going around chasing their tails. They thought it was somebody from Sligo Town. Then they thought it was somebody from the local area. They haven't a bloody clue. They will never find out who is responsible, not unless the fecker has a conscience and owns up himself. That's the only way they will get the bastard." Ollie seemed very sure of his sources. He would be getting gossip and information on his travels around Sligo and Galway.

Conor again thought of Darragh and wondered if he had given himself up yet in a Garda station in Galway city. What was he doing now? Was he lying in a cell, feeling that his life was over, or did he feel relieved that he had finally confessed?

Thanks to the chatty driver, the remaining hour's journey to Rathalgin went quick. Conor's father was waiting for him in his car at the bus stop. The chat on the way home between Conor and his dad was about how the snow had all disappeared fierce quick, but how there was much more heavier snow promised in the coming days.

Conor didn't tell his father about what Darragh had confessed to, even though he wanted to. He didn't know what to do. If Darragh had not given himself up, should he tell the Gardai himself?

When Conor got home, his mother had his dinner in the oven. He ate it and sat down for a while in the sitting room, but he couldn't relax. He told his parents that he felt wrecked after a rough night in Galway and that he was going for a few hours' kip upstairs in bed.

He lay in the darkened room on his single bed for a few hours, but he couldn't sleep. He thought about going for a few drinks in Sheehan's to help him sleep.

Just as he was thinking about it, he heard the phone ringing in the hallway downstairs. His mother answered it and shouted up the stairs, "Conor, a call for you."

"Okay Mam, tell them I'll be down in a second," Conor replied. He went downstairs to answer the phone.

It was Sarah.

"Hi Sarah, how are you? Did you survive the blizzard?" Conor asked mockingly.

"Yea, just about. Look, I'm just ringing to ask if you want to come up to watch a film or something. I got a video recorder as a Christmas present from my dad and I haven't a feckin' clue how to hook it up. It's been sitting in a box for the last week. I was thinking for my New Year's resolution to give up the booze and maybe watch a few videos at home instead. I even rented out a video today."

"What did you get? I suppose, knowing your rotten taste in films, it's probably *'Dirty Dancing'* or some other tripe."

"No, actually, you cheeky bastard, it's *'Midnight Run'*, with Robert de Niro," Sarah replied.

"That's a fun movie. Good choice. I went to see it in the cinema in London. It's a good laugh."

"See, I told you I could pick a good film. I'm not just a pretty face. I'll call down for you; you can't be borrowing your dad's car all the time. Oh yea—bring some popcorn." Sarah laughed.

"Right," Conor said, "give me an hour. See you then."

He put down the phone, went up to the bathroom, had a shower and changed his clothes.

Sarah picked him up at around eight and they headed back out to Rossbeg. There were still plenty of Garda cars patrolling the area. They still appeared to be searching around houses and farmyards. Conor wondered if the bus driver had been correct when he'd said that they could not trace the burnt out car to Tom Kearns's killer. The fact that the Garda cars were still searching around could mean that Darragh had not given himself up earlier this morning.

"So when are you back at work?" Conor asked.

"I am back on the fifth, I think. What day is it today? You get so feckin' mixed up about what day it even is over Christmas," Sarah replied as she lit a fag with the car cigarette lighter and blew the smoke out the window.

"I think it's Monday." Conor laughed. "So you're back on Thursday."

"Yea, Thursday." Sarah sighed. "I hate the thought of going back to that bloody shithole of a bank. When are you going back to work in England? Or are you going back?"

"My flight back is next Saturday. I'm back at work next Monday," Conor replied.

"What are you working at? I think you told me last week, but I can't remember," Sarah said.

"It's a company called Castle Insurance. We do car and home insurance."

"Do you like it?"

"Yea, it's okay. I got promoted to section manager last November," Conor said with a grin.

"Oooh, aren't you the lucky boy." Sarah laughed. "Fancy Conor Doyle from Ballinastrad, a manager. A section manager for Castle Insurance in London no less, wowee."

"Stop taking the piss," Conor responded.

He and Sarah had always gotten on well. They shared a similar sense of humour and they enjoyed winding each other up.

After a short journey, Sarah pulled her car up outside the front door of her home. She got out of the car and opened the front door. Conor followed her inside.

"Well, take your coat off, Conor," Sarah said. Conor took off his coat and hung it beside the door. "The video player is in the box on the table. I'll make a pot of tea. Are you hungry?"

"No, I'm grand, Sarah, thanks," Conor replied.

After taking the VCR out of the cardboard box, he placed it beside the TV up on the shelf next to the window. He connected the leads from the VCR to the TV and after studying the instruction manual for a while, he managed to tune it in after four or five attempts and several outbursts of expletives.

Sarah and Conor sat down on the couch and watched the video she had rented. They shared a bottle of red wine and enjoyed the comedy and each other's company. Conor was trying hard to forget about Darragh and what he had told him.

He probably should tell Sarah about it. In fact, he thought, he should really tell the Gardai about it if Darragh hadn't already. But then he would be grassing on his best friend. What was the right thing to do? His mind was in overdrive.

When the movie was over, the pair sat and chatted for a time and both of them avoided bringing up Darragh's name. It had been a long day and despite the fact that he was so happy to be sharing time with Sarah, Conor was mentally exhausted. He began to find it difficult to keep his eyes open and eventually, he drifted into a snooze in front of the warm fire.

"Some company you are, Conor Doyle." Sarah laughed as she elbowed him in the side.

"Sorry, it must be the wine. It always makes me sleepy. And the heat in here—it's bloody roasting."

"Look, you better stay. I'm not able to drive you back into town after drinking and there are checkpoints all over the place," Sarah said as she cleared up glasses from the coffee table.

"Okay. I'll stay in the spare room," Conor replied.

"You don't have to, Conor. I find it hard to sleep on my own," Sarah said, grabbing Conor by the arm. "Go on down to my room. I'll be down in a few minutes; I'll just tidy up."

Conor walked down the hall to Sarah and Darragh's bedroom. After getting undressed, he got in under the cold sheets and shivered for a few moments. He could hear Sarah washing glasses and mugs in the kitchen.

He lay there for a few moments and surveyed the bedroom. Some of Darragh's clothes and other possessions were scattered around the room. His brown and battered ex-army boots were sitting under a chair next to the bed and an old pair of paint-spattered Wrangler jeans were wrapped in a ball in the corner of the room next to the wardrobe. Two of his abstract paintings hung on the walls.

Guilt overcame Conor. He felt rotten to be sleeping in Darragh's bed and soon with Darragh's girlfriend. He turned his head over on the pillow to try to blot out all the mixed emotions that were going on in his head.

Sarah came into the room ten minutes later and got into bed beside him. She wrapped her arms around him and the two of them lay close together, holding each other. After a few minutes, he could hear Sarah drifting off to sleep. He looked over at the digital clock radio. It was 12.44.

Chapter XI

Riders on the Storm

Tuesday, 3rd January 1989

Darragh looked at his watch; it was 12.05 am. He was parked on the main street in Ballinastrad. The town looked very quiet. Only five or six cars were parked along the street. Sheehan's Pub looked like it was closed; all the lights were out. The Christmas buzz was over and Ballinastrad had settled back into its usual quiet slumber.

He lit a cigarette and replayed the events of the previous twenty-four hours in his mind. He recalled talking to Conor in the hotel front bar in the early hours of the morning in Galway and how Conor had convinced him to go to the Gardai to come clean. He'd laid in bed in his hotel room contemplating what to do. He had decided that he must face the consequences alone and leave the hotel before Conor got up so that his friend would be spared the embarrassment of accompanying him to confess his crime. After checking out of the Waterfront Hotel at 9.30 in the morning, he'd walked towards the nearest Garda station to get some relief for his heavy and troubled conscience.

However, he had just not been able to motivate himself to walk up the steps and in through the doorway to the front desk to begin the process. He'd hung around outside the Garda station for nearly half an hour trying to bring himself to take the short journey inside. Each time, he'd just bottled out. He'd known that once he took those steps through the doors, his life would change forever. He would become the focus of ridicule, hatred and bitterness.

He'd gone into a nearby bar and ordered a whiskey to settle his nerves and give him the false courage to try again to enter the Garda station. One drink had turned into too many.

The more he'd drunk, the more he'd thought that perhaps there were other options. Maybe he could move away to the US and start again. Maybe he could in some way bury the flashbacks to the killing of Tom Kearns.

His thoughts had turned to the people closest to him; how could he leave them behind? His mother and sister in Sligo Town and Sarah back in Ballinastrad. He'd decided that he would have to see them, to say goodbye to his family and make peace with Sarah.

Maybe he could convince Sarah to come with him to America. They'd often thought about it. Sarah had an older brother called Paul in Boston. He'd often invited them over. He'd said he could fix them up with jobs. They were both tired and fed up with Ballinastrad; it was time to get away, while they were still young.

The more Darragh had thought about it, the more he'd convinced himself that it was the best option. It was a moment of vivid clarity; he knew what he would do now. He had a clear plan. He would go and see his sister and his mother first and then he would go home to Sarah and begin to pack his things and organise the flights to Boston. A day or two would sort it out. The two of them could be in Boston by the weekend. A new year and a new start: a new life.

He finished off his drink and headed for the bus station. He only had to wait twenty minutes for the next bus to Sligo Town. He arrived in Sligo at two o'clock in the afternoon and got a taxi to his sister's house on the Strandhill Road out of Sligo Town.

His sister Anne was surprised to see him. She lived in the opulent end of town in a large house overlooking the bay. She was married to a doctor who worked in the hospital. She had two young children who were delighted to see Darragh, as he always acted the big kid with them.

Darragh's mother lived only a mile down along the bay and Anne had rung her to come over to her house, as Darragh was there. The three of them shared a meal together and Darragh told his mother and sister about his plans.

"I have decided to immigrate to America. To Boston."

Anne and her mother smiled over at one another; they didn't take the plan too seriously, as they knew that Darragh wouldn't be able to hold down a job over in America because he would be too lazy to get up in the morning.

"Oh, really? When did you come up with this idea, Darragh?" Anne asked as she took a mouthful of red wine.

"I have been thinking about it for a few months. Sarah and I are planning to go."

"Will Sarah give up her job in the bank?" Mrs Lonigan asked.

"Yea, she said she is tired of it. Sarah's brother in Boston is going to set us up for a while," Darragh replied.

"What are you going to work at in Boston? You don't really have any practical skills. You won't make a living as an artist," Mrs Lonigan said.

"I might do. Anyway, I'll work at anything for a year or so. Maybe I'll work at construction. I'm not fussy. I could turn my hand to lots of things."

Darragh's mother and sister assumed that he would be in Boston for a month or so, then run out of money and be back home with his tail between his legs. However, they wouldn't stand in his way. Maybe it might make him realise what the real world was all about and help him to mature.

"Look, if you want to go, you should go. I spent some time in America when I was a younger woman. I worked there during the summers when I was in university many years ago. America is an inspiring place. Have you money for air fare?" Mrs Lonigan asked as she reached for her handbag.

"Well, sort of," Darragh stuttered.

"I take it that means no. Here's something to cover the air fare and also a bit extra to tide you over for a few months," Mrs Lonigan said as she wrote out a cheque and handed it to Darragh.

"Thanks, Mum. I promise that I will send back the money in a few weeks once I get working."

His mother nodded, smiled and said, "Sure, Darragh, no problem," as she winked over at her daughter.

"By the way, Anne, I was wondering: could I ask you a favour? Could I borrow your car for a day or two so I can drive back to the cottage in Rossbeg to start packing my things?" Darragh asked.

"What happened to your own car?"

"A long story. It's giving me a bit of trouble. It's in the garage getting fixed."

"I suppose you can take the Golf. But look after it. The last time I gave you a car, you reversed it into a wall. I'll get you the keys."

"You're a life-saver, sis. I will drop it back to you safe and sound with a full tank of petrol in two days' time."

"It's a diesel, by the way." Anne laughed.

Darragh spent the rest of the day at his sister's house, and in the evening, he said good luck to his mother, sister, and two nephews and drove off.

On the way towards Ballinastrad, he stopped off in Castlederry for a few stiff drinks again to boost his spirits before he got home to Sarah to try to charm her into his plans for moving to Boston.

As he sat in Greegan's Bar, he watched the nine o'clock news. One of the news stories mentioned that Gardai in Sligo had discovered fresh information in relation to the death of Tom Kearns in a recent hit-and-run incident near the village of Ballinastrad. A Garda spokesperson said that they had now narrowed down their investigation after discovering key evidence that would help to find the individual responsible in the coming days. They also issued a plea for anybody with information that could help the investigation further to contact the Garda station in Sligo Town. A phone number was read out.

Darragh wondered what had they discovered. He had torched his Toyota and made sure to remove the number plates first. He had thrown the number plates into the flooded quarry hole nearby. Had the Gardai found a chassis number or something else that might lead them to him?

Anyway, it was just another burnt-out car. It didn't mean that it was involved in the hit-and-run.

Sweat was now beading on Darragh's forehead. He was beginning to doubt his plan to go to Boston with Sarah. Maybe it was too late. Maybe the Garda noose was already tightening around him. Perhaps Conor was right; perhaps he should give himself up.

No, he thought, he had to see Sarah. He had to make things right. He would tell her the truth about what had happened and she would advise him on what to do.

He had a couple more drinks and headed for Ballinastrad. He stayed off the main roads to avoid Garda checkpoints. The long detour meant that he didn't arrive in Ballinastrad until after twelve o'clock.

He drove slowly up and down Main Street and Bridge Street to see if Sarah's car was parked anywhere. He drove past Sheehan's, O'Brien's and Dolan's to no avail. He would have to drive out to their house in Rossbeg.

Darragh hoped that the Gardai were not at his house already. It was probably a foolish idea to go back there but if he was going to leave the country, he would need his passport and that was in the house someplace.

Darragh crept slowly out the side roads from Bridge Street towards Rossbeg. Fortunately, he came across no Garda checkpoints or random patrols.

It was raining very heavy as Darragh got closer to the cottage that he shared with Sarah. The house was part of a large one hundred acre farm of land that had belonged to his father, James Lonigan. The farm was leased out now to different local farmers and the rent Darragh had collected from it just before Christmas helped to keep him in beer money for a few months. After that, he had to survive on whatever he could make from selling paintings, and also, of course, handouts from his wealthy mother, who was still a practicing solicitor.

The Lonigans had always been the big shouts in the area. James Lonigan had owned several large farms of land. He had also been the local undertaker, a publican and of course, a long-serving county councillor. James Lonigan had been a good man to have on your side, the kind of man who'd had the power to pull strings, as the saying goes. He could get you planning permission for a roller disco in a bird sanctuary, if the bribe was right.

He'd been about to get a shot at the big time just before he died. He was on the verge of getting the Fianna Fáil County Cumman's nomination to run as a TD in the next general election. However, he'd suffered a massive heart attack and dropped dead behind the bar of his pub at the relatively young age of 49.

Darragh had only been 23 at the time and his mother felt that he should have followed his late father into politics. His county council seat would have been secured for him in the general fashion of nepotism that is characteristic of Irish politics.

However, Darragh had had other plans. He was going to set the world alight as an artist and had no time for vulgar politics. Darragh saw himself as an intellectual, an artist, a lover, a boozer and a brawler, the classic drunken Irish artist. Darragh believed his own bullshit and expected everybody else to do likewise.

The rain was beating so hard on the windscreen that Darragh was forced to stop because the window wipers on his sister's Volkswagen Golf couldn't clear the deluge. He lit a cigarette and waited for the rain to ease before he drove on. He was only about a quarter of a mile away from the house.

He thought about what he would say to Sarah when he went inside. He decided to write a note for her just in case she wouldn't listen to him. Maybe if she read the note afterwards, she might change her mind. He thought about where he would go if she wouldn't let him stay. She couldn't be heartless enough to put him out on a night like this, could she?

He found a notebook and a pen in the glove compartment of the car and wrote to Sarah.

Sarah,

You probably hate me right now, and I don't blame you at all. You have been nothing but loving and kind to me over the last eight years that we have been together. You put up with my ignorance, my rudeness, my drunkenness, and my unfaithfulness. You have been so patient and forgiving to me over the years. I just want to say to you that I love you deeply. I can't live without you. I would rather be dead than to lose you, Sarah. You are my life. Without you, life is pointless.

Darragh knew that it sounded a bit corny, but it might just work. He folded up the note and put it in his inside coat pocket.

After about twenty minutes, the heavy rain began to lessen and he drove on towards the house. Sarah's car was parked outside and all the lights inside the house were turned out.

He decided not to knock on the front door. Instead, he got the spare key that was hidden under a cavity block at the back of the hayshed in the farmyard at the side of the house. After getting soaking wet in the process of finding the key in the dark, he walked towards the front door of the house and quietly opened it. He didn't turn on the kitchen light, instead taking off his wet coat and putting it on the back of a chair next to the fire to dry.

He opened the hall door and walked down towards the main bedroom, where he hoped to find Sarah sleeping. The bedroom door was ajar and he crept in quietly. It was pitch dark in the bedroom; all he could see was the digital alarm clock. It was 1.17 in the morning.

Darragh sat on the bed. He began whispering quietly to Sarah saying how sorry he was about what had happened and that he hoped that she would have the heart to forgive him one last time. He kept talking, but there was no reply.

He leaned over on the bed; he could feel the outline of her ankle under the sheets. He shook her ankle gently, trying to wake her. After a minute she gave a slight groan and babbled, half-asleep, "What's wrong? What's wrong?"

"Sarah, Sarah. It's me, Darragh."

"What? Who?" Sarah asked. "Darragh? Darragh, Christ." Sarah pulled her legs up under the sheets and reached over to turn on the bedside lamp. "Darragh? Is that you, Darragh?"

As the lamp illuminated the bedroom, there was silence for a moment and then Darragh roared, "Fuck you, Sarah, you haven't been wasting anytime, have you? Who is the bastard in the bed next to you?"

"Just get out, Darragh. You had no right to come in here. Get out."

In a rage, Darragh flung the blankets and sheets off the bed, revealing Conor on the other side of the double bed. His mouth dropped.

"Conor." He could barely speak after the shock. Then his rage returned. "Conor, you treacherous fuckin' scumbag. How could you, Conor? You bloody bastard."

Conor jumped out of bed and pulled on his t-shirt and jeans. Darragh was in a frenzy; throwing boots, chairs and his own paintings around the room as he roared and sobbed. Tears ran down his cheeks and his face was molten red with rage. The veins were pumping in his neck and his eyes were bulging as if they were going to explode.

"You pair of treacherous fuckers," he roared. "Sarah, you bitch. Conor, I'll rip your fucking head off, you dirty bastard."

Conor tried to reason with him, but Darragh levelled him with a blow to the side of the jaw that propelled him against the wardrobe. Darragh pulled Conor up again off the floor and pounded him viciously several more times.

Sarah was screaming. "Darragh, stop it! Stop it! Just get out."

He turned around to face her, his face still raging. He stared at her with a look not just of hatred, but also of despair and disappointment. He pushed her to one side and stormed out of the bedroom and out the front door.

Sarah could hear his car revving and breaks screeching as he tore off down the road. She went over to where Conor was lying next to the wardrobe. His nose was pumping blood. She ran to the bathroom and brought back a towel to clean up some of the blood.

"Are you okay, Conor?" she asked.

"Yea, I'm okay. I'm okay."

She helped him onto the bed. She placed his head on the pillow as she tried to clean his wounds.

"I think I should bring you to a hospital, Conor."

"No, seriously, Sarah, don't be fussing. I'm really not that bad. Nothing's broken; I don't think so, anyway. It probably looks much worse than it really is."

After the bleeding had stopped and Sarah had cleaned up his face, she got dressed and went back to the kitchen and locked and bolted the front door.

"I probably should go after him to see if he is okay," Conor said.

"You will not. The state he is in, if you catch up with him, he will probably kill you," Sarah said sternly. "Get some rest, Conor. We will try to catch up with him tomorrow when he calms down. No doubt he will be drowning his sorrows in Sheehan's."

Chapter XII

Running to Standstill

Tuesday, 3ʳᵈ January 1989

Conor lay back on the pillow. His head was pounding and his nose was throbbing. After an hour or so, he drifted off to sleep.

He woke up early in the afternoon; the clock beside his bed read 12.55. Sarah wasn't next to him; he presumed she had gotten up earlier. He got up and dressed and went into the bathroom to survey how bad he looked in the mirror.

The cuts on his face from the thumping he got from Darragh were still stinging. His nose was red and swollen, and his top lip was busted. He threw cold water up onto his face in an effort to sooth the pain. It gave him a temporary relief.

Then he went into the kitchen. Sarah was sitting at the table smoking a fag and drinking a mug of coffee.

"Are you up long?" he asked.

"What … I never went to bed. I stayed up. I couldn't sleep." She was in a trance-like daze staring at the floor.

She lifted her eyes up and asked Conor if he was okay. He told her that he felt fine. He got a glass of water and sat down beside her at the table.

"That bastard Darragh was in some rage. He's a fuckin' lunatic. I never seen him like that before," Sarah said.

"Yea, he was bloody crazy, but I suppose he was angry to catch us in bed together. His best friend and his girlfriend. I suppose in one way you can't blame him," Conor responded as he tried to drink the glass of water from the side of his mouth that didn't hurt.

Sarah gave a piercing glance at Conor. "Jesus Christ, you can't be serious. You are not going to defend that psycho, are you? He could have bloody killed you," she snapped.

"He has a lot on his mind. He's fucked up," Conor shouted back.

"What the hell has he got to worry about with his rich mammy looking after him? All he has to worry about is the next drink and the next piece of skirt he's going to pick up. I should have dropped him years ago, the amount of times that rat was with other women! He probably had them here, for fuck sake, when I went home some weekends to Donegal, or even when I was at work. Who knows? Nothing would surprise me with Darragh Lonigan."

Conor decided not to respond. He let Sarah blow off some steam. He knew it was pointless arguing with her and trying to defend Darragh. He went over towards her and held her close. Her rage turned to tears and she sobbed relentlessly on his shoulder.

They ate breakfast and began to talk calmly about what needed to be said. They talked about where Darragh might have gone. Sarah said that he had friends about five miles away in Shemore; he could have stayed with them last night.

"This morning he was either drinking someplace, maybe in Ballinastrad or in some other nearby town, or he might have gone to stay with his sister in Strandhill. He often went over there. He enjoyed spending time with her two boys."

Conor assumed that Darragh had not given himself up to the Gardai. He needed to tell somebody about Darragh's confession to him. The burden of this knowledge was weighing heavy on Conor's mind. He felt he needed to tell Sarah, but she was already so traumatised by what had happened that he didn't want to upset her any more. As Conor and Sarah sat on the couch they heard a car driving over the gravel entrance outside the house. "Maybe it's Darragh," said Sarah as she quickly stood up and walked over to the kitchen window

Conor got up and joined her by the window. As he looked out through the dusty pane, he realised that it was a Garda car. A plain clothes detective got out of the passenger seat and walked towards the front door and knocked hard.

Sarah wrapped her long grey cardigan around her and answered the door. The middle aged detective held up his identification and introduced himself as Detective Mulcahy.

"Hi miss, I think we were speaking the other morning. You're Sarah? Sarah Gallagher?" the detective asked.

"Oh yes, that's right. Come in, detective. How can I help you?" Sarah responded nervously.

The detective came in and immediately looked over at Conor sitting at the table. He noticed the cuts and bruises on his face.

"Can I ask who you are, sir?" Detective Mulcahy asked.

"I'm Conor Doyle. I live in Ballinastrad. I'm just an old college friend of Sarah's."

"Okay, Conor. You don't look too good. What happened to your face, if you don't mind me asking?"

Conor paused for a moment. "I fell off my bicycle yesterday. I went out for a cycle. I wasn't used to the bike, came down a hill too fast and bam, hit a pothole. It threw me right off the bike and I cut my face as I grazed it against the road."

"You were lucky you didn't do yourself worse harm," Jim Mulcahy said. He walked towards a chair beside the fireplace. "Do you mind if I sit down?"

"Sure, please, sit down," Sarah replied.

He unbuttoned his coat as he sat down. "The last time I called here, you told me that there was another man living here called Darragh Lonigan."

"That's right." Sarah didn't say much. Conor thought she probably wanted to avoid answering any awkward questions about Darragh's whereabouts.

"Well, we are trying to locate him. As you know, we are still carrying out our investigations into the violent and tragic death of Tom Kearns. Recently we found a burnt-out car, the remains of a blue Toyota Starlet, beside an abandoned quarry near Rathalgin. This may or may not be linked to the aforementioned Tom Kearns incident. However, as you might understand, we are trying to follow any possible leads and if we could talk to Mr Lonigan, we could rule out that particular line of enquiry. Is he at work? Is he due back shortly? Do you know where we could locate him?"

Sarah clearly felt awkward and uncomfortable, as though she didn't know what to tell the detective.

"I'm sorry, I don't know where he is," she muttered.

Detective Mulcahy was silent and stared over at Sarah. Then he said, "Sarah, according to information we have received, Mr Lonigan and yourself have been cohabiting here for the last two years. We have been told that you are a couple. He is your long-term ... boyfriend. Surely you must have some idea where he is and when he is likely to come back."

"I'm sorry, I don't know where he is," Sarah repeated.

Conor felt sorry for Sarah. He could see the way the questioning was going and he felt ashamed that he knew the truth and that he had not told her.

Detective Mulcahy then turned to Conor, sensing that he was becoming uncomfortable. "Conor, you are a friend of Sarah's, as you told me earlier. Do you know Darragh well?"

"Yes, the three of us went to college together. We've been close friends for many years. I've known Darragh since we were kids," Conor replied nervously.

The detective leaned forward in his chair. "So I take it you have visited this house on a number of occasions."

"I have only visited the house here two or three times over the last two weeks since I came home for holidays," Conor said, looking over at Sarah.

"Perhaps you can help me then, Conor. What kind of car does Darragh drive? Is it perhaps a blue Toyota Starlet? A five-door hatchback?" Detective Mulcahy asked.

Conor paused for a moment. Had he any choice now but to disclose information that would lead the detective fairly rapidly to an obvious conclusion, or should he just tell him what Darragh had confessed to him and avoid all the unnecessary bullshit?

Jim Mulcahy was becoming impatient. "Conor, did your friend Darragh Lonigan drive a blue Toyota Starlet?"

"Yes, yes he did."

"And where is that car now? Have you seen it lately?"

"No, I haven't seen it in a few days."

"When did you last see the car? Conor, please try to be as specific and accurate as you can."

Suddenly Sarah interjected. "Where is all this going? How do you know it was Darragh's Toyota? It could have been anybody's; it's a fairly common make of car."

"So Sarah, getting back to you then—when is the last time you seen Darragh driving the Toyota?"

"I'm not sure. Maybe just before Christmas Day. He was driving mine for a few days over the holidays; he said his car was giving him trouble. I think there was a massive dinge on it. He said he was going to get it fixed or scrap it and buy another one. Darragh was always buying cheap bangers of cars and replacing them every six months or so. It was hard to keep track of what he was driving."

The detective seemed to realise he was getting somewhere. "Would it be possible that he began talking about getting rid of the Toyota around about the 22nd of December and that you might have noticed the large ding on it around about the same time?"

"Yes, I suppose so. Hold on, are you implying that Darragh was responsible for the hit-and-run? Oh God, that can't be true. No way." Sarah was becoming hysterical.

Conor stood up. "Can't you leave her? Can't you see she is upset?"

Jim Mulcahy sat back in his chair. "Look, I'm sorry. I'm just trying to avoid giving yourself and Sarah as much grief as possible. I could have brought you both to the local station, but I wanted to spare you from that stress for the moment."

Conor got Sarah, the detective and himself a cup of coffee each and they sat quietly for a few minutes. Jim Mulcahy was the first to break the silence.

"Look, we know already that the burnt-out Toyota starlet that was found near Rathalgin quite possibly belongs to Darragh Lonigan. It was well burnt-out and the number plates were removed. We couldn't find any chassis numbers or serial numbers anywhere on the body. They must have been filed down or destroyed by the blaze. Whoever did the work was determined that the car wouldn't be traced back to them. However, we did discover only yesterday, in the ditch in the corner of the field where the car was burnt-out, a ripped-up ESB bill with Darragh's name and this address on it. Perhaps he ripped it up himself and disposed of it in the ditch. Maybe it was under a car seat and he forgot to remove it before torching the car and it blew out the door of that car at some point. Now, perhaps the ESB bill has no link with the car, but why would a utility bill belonging to Darragh be found in a field over twenty miles from here? Possibly he tossed it out his car window at some stage as he drove by that area."

"Now, obviously it's not a great piece of evidence. It might mean nothing. But it's all a bit too coincidental. A blue Toyota Starlet is burned out in a field. An ESB bill is found close by belonging to Darragh. He was driving a blue Toyota Starlet up until the time the car was found burnt-out. To add to that, you have just told me, Sarah, that you noticed that the car was damaged sometime after the 21st of December. It looked to you like the car collided with

117

something, maybe a ditch? Look, Sarah, you can see how this is adding up.

"We need to talk to Darragh. It's possible that he had a crash with the car and he had nothing to do with the hit-and-run incident. We just need to interview him to see if we can rule out this particular line of enquiry. You told me earlier you don't know where he is, Sarah. Is that true? Look, think about it; I'm going outside for a few minutes to talk to my colleagues."

Jim Mulcahy opened the kitchen door and went outside. He got into the Garda car and talked to another detective in the backseat of the car and two uniformed Gardai in the front seats.

Sarah looked over at Conor. "Do you think there is any link between Darragh and the hit-and-run, the killing of that poor man, Tom Kearns?"

Conor did not know what to say. Should he tell her the truth? He felt he couldn't keep in the secret anymore. He sat there, silently and nervously staring out the window.

"Conor. Conor, will you say something? What do you think, or are you as shocked and stunned as I am?"

"I don't know, Sarah. I don't know what to say." Conor couldn't hold onto the heavy burden any longer. "I think it's true. I think it's possible."

Sarah looked at him, puzzled. "How can you be so sure, Conor? Do you know something more about this? Did he tell you about what happened?"

"Yes, yes," Conor whispered weakly. "He told me."

"He told you what? What did he tell you? When did he tell you?" Sarah was getting hysterical again.

"He told me early yesterday morning in Galway. I was going to tell you, but I couldn't seem to find the right words or the right time. I felt like I was betraying him. Oh God, I don't know what I felt."

"He rang me New Year's Eve around the same time you rang. He told me he was in Galway City and he asked me to come over and meet him on New Year's Day. I went over and we had a good bit to drink. In the bar of the hotel we were staying in, he confessed to me that he had knocked down Tom Kearns and driven off and left him dying on the road."

"Look, I wanted to tell you, to tell somebody. I'm sorry. I was going to tell you this morning, or afternoon, whatever bloody time it is. I told Darragh to give himself up to the local Garda station in Galway city. He promised me that he would the next morning, but when I got up, he had checked out of the hotel and was gone. That's as much as I know, Sarah."

Sarah starting crying. Conor could hear her mumbling to herself, "Oh Darragh, oh Darragh. Why, why? How could he do that? I hate you for how you mistreated me and lied to me so many times and I hate you for leaving that poor man to die, but I loved you, Darragh. I fuckin' loved you so much for so long and now your life is ruined."

Sarah was crying for herself and for Darragh. Her beautiful young face appeared to age in those short few minutes. Conor gave her a hanky and she wiped her eyes and diverted them towards him. "You will have to tell the detective what you just told me, Conor."

"Yes, yes. I suppose I have to," Conor replied.

There was a knock on the door. Conor got up from his chair and let Detective Mulcahy in. This time, he was accompanied by a young uniformed Guard. They both sat at the table. The young Garda took out a notebook and prepared himself to record details.

Jim Mulcahy noticed that Sarah had been crying. "Are you okay, Sarah? Is there anything wrong? You look upset. I'm sorry if you find all of this distressing."

"I'm fine. I'm okay."

"Now Sarah, I will try to get through this quickly. Is there anything more you can tell me? I appreciate your cooperation so far. You have been very helpful. I understand how hard this is on you. I know yourself and Darragh are very close."

Conor nervously interrupted. "There is something I need to tell you, Mr Mulcahy." He retold the events surrounding Darragh's confession to him in Galway.

Jim Mulcahy looked at the young Garda to check that he was recording the information. He then turned to Conor and in an angry outburst, he shouted, "You have known this information for over twenty-four hours. Why did you not inform the Gardai before this?"

"As I said, Darragh had promised me that he would go to the Gardai himself yesterday morning. I had no idea when I left Galway yesterday whether he had given himself up or not. I assumed he had until last night."

"What happened last night?" Jim Mulcahy asked.

Conor was silent. He looked over at Sarah and she nodded at him as if wanting him to tell the truth about what had happened.

"He ... he came back here last night or early this morning. I suppose it was around one AM. Myself and Sarah were sharing a bed. He thought that something was going on between us and he went crazy and started smashing up the bedroom. He left after I suppose fifteen minutes when Sarah told him to leave."

"I see. Is that how you got those bruises on your face?" the detective asked.

"Yea," replied Conor.

"So where do you think Darragh is now? Where would he have stayed when he left here last night?"

"I'm really not sure," Sarah replied. "He might have driven to Strandhill in Sligo to stay with his sister Anne, or he has friends living a few miles up the road in Shemore, Eoin and Oliver Casey. He stayed over with them sometimes; they were drinking buddies. Maybe he stayed in one of the properties belonging to his family. His mother owns property all over the place. She has flats in Sligo Town and student houses in Cartron. I think she has a house in Lismore as well. Darragh might have had keys for any of them."

"You said his sister was called Anne. Have you a phone number for her?" Jim Mulcahy asked.

"Yea, I have it somewhere," Sarah said as she got up to root about in a cupboard.

"Oh and also, have you any photographs? Recent ones of Darragh, please. It would really help."

"Okay," Sarah said. "I'll see what I can find."

After searching for about fifteen minutes, Sarah found in a drawer a notebook that contained phone numbers of family members and friends. She also found a number of photographs of Darragh. Some of them were photos of the two of them taken on a holiday in Edinburgh the previous summer.

Conor watched as she stared at the photos for a few minutes, tears in her eyes. She also found Darragh's passport. She handed the items to Detective Mulcahy.

"Thanks very much, Sarah. Again, you have been most cooperative. And thanks to you as well, Conor, for your information, even if it was a little late forthcoming."

"What happens now?" Sarah asked.

"Well, we will have to try to locate Darragh and when we find him, bring him in for questioning and see what happens from there. We will need both of you to come to a Garda station in the near future so we can fill out official details on the report. I think it's wise if we leave a Garda car in close proximity in case Darragh decides to return here. I hope that is okay."

"Yes, that's fine," Sarah replied.

"Okay, that's it. As I said, there will be a Garda car outside your home, so if you want to contact me, just tell the lads in the patrol car and they can radio me."

When the detective and the young Guard had left, Sarah and Conor sat in silence for a few minutes before Conor asked, "Do you want me to stay with you for a while? I don't think you should be on your own."

"Yea, please, I could do with the company. Do you want me to drive you in to Ballinastrad to collect a few things, if you want to stay over?" Sarah asked.

"That would be good. I could do with a shower to freshen up and a change of clothes."

After a quick wash, Sarah drove her Ford Mondeo out of the front entrance of the yard and headed towards Ballinastrad. A Garda patrol car was parked at a laneway facing the house. It was twenty past three on a cold, dark and damp January Day.

Chapter XIII

Into the Mystic

Wednesday, 4th January 1989

Sarah and Conor had spent much of the evening tidying the bedroom from the damage that was caused in the early hours of the previous morning. Both of them had tried to function as best they could, but as much as they tried, their thoughts kept returning to Darragh and his whereabouts.

After rising in the early morning, unable to sleep, they decided to go for a walk. A Garda car remained just outside the house and observed them as they travelled down the road.

It was a bright, clear and frosty morning. The sky was a vibrant blue overhead. It was cold, but the air felt fresh and clean. As Sarah and Conor walked over the hills of Rossbeg, there was a perfect view of the calm waters of Lough Oughter below. Despite the cold conditions, small rowing boats were dotted around the waters. Further on in the distance, a network of lanes and roads intertwined like a web and the towns and villages of Rathalgin, Ballinastrad, and Castlederry could be seen.

The hills of Rossbeg were the highest points in the parish and from here, a person felt like an old Celtic chieftain surveying his lands. It was certainly a mystical place, with an ancient Neolithic Portal Dolmen, a Bronze Age stone circle and the remains of a Crannog in the centre of Lough Oughter. Sarah pointed some of the landmarks out to Conor as they strolled. He could see why Sarah and Darragh had chosen to live there. It certainly was a beautiful and captivating place on a bright, clear day.

Conor remembered coming up to the Rossbeg Hills with Darragh and Darragh's father when they were kids. He also remembered coming to the ringfort on the land beside Darragh and Sarah's cottage. It was tradition to have a picnic there on every Easter Monday. All the kids from the area would congregate in the ringfort and light a bonfire. He wasn't sure the significance of that particular day; supposedly it was a tradition that went on for hundreds of years previous.

All of these memories made him wonder if Darragh was someplace below them in the villages or houses or if he had now departed many miles away to another part of the country. Maybe he had crossed over to Britain. Maybe the Guards had located him already.

After the walk, Sarah and Conor returned to the house. They felt a bit better after getting some fresh air. They cooked a meal and as they sat at the table, Sarah noticed the black coat that belonged to Darragh hanging on the back of the chair next to the fire.

"How long has that coat been there?" she asked.

"That has been there since yesterday, I think. It was on the floor behind the chair yesterday evening. I think I remember picking it up and placing it on the back of the chair when we were tidying up."

There were coats and other clothes of Darragh's lying all around the kitchen area. Sarah was in no way a domestic goddess and did not seem too interested in keeping the living area particularly tidy.

"That's the coat that Darragh was wearing for the last week or so. I think he bought it in a second-hand clothes shop in Sligo a few weeks before Christmas."

Sarah went over and picked up the coat and searched through the pockets. She found a box of matches and a pack of cigarettes in one pocket and in the other inside pocket, a piece of note paper. Conor could see that it was addressed to her.

She read the note slowly. The handwriting was Darragh's typical scrawl but his words caused her to burst into tears. She kept reading the final lines out loud over and over again.

"I can't live without you. I would rather be dead than lose you. Sarah, you are my life. Without you, life is pointless."

Conor went over to her and held her.

"Oh God, Conor, what does this mean? Is it a suicide note? What does it mean?" she screamed hysterically.

Conor tried his best to console her and tried to convince her that Darragh would never take that way out. However, as he said it, in his own mind, he thought it was a possibility. Maybe Darragh felt he had nothing now to live for. He had lost his girlfriend and his best friend and he knew that once he was caught by the Gardai or if he gave himself up, his life was as good as over anyway.

The other explanation for the note was that it was just a sick attempt by Darragh to try to win Sarah back. He had often convinced Sarah to take him back in the past by attempting similar stunts. On one occasion when they lived in Galway, Sarah had discovered that Darragh had been unfaithful to her and broken it off with him. He had threatened to jump into the sea in Salthill and drown himself unless she would take him back. It had worked.

Darragh was always very dramatic and he liked to play the tortured and troubled artist at times. Perhaps that was why he drank so much. He had a romantic notion of himself as the drunken Irish artist living in the remote hills of Sligo, just like all the other writers, poets and artists who moved to the west of Ireland to find inspiration to feed their creative souls.

Darragh had often talked about how all the greats 'checked out', as he called it, at twenty seven: Brian Jones, Jimi Hendrix, Janis Joplin and his hero, Jim Morrison. The mythical 27 club. Darragh and Conor had travelled to Paris together back in 1985 and had visited the grave of Jim Morrison in Père Lachaise Cemetery. Darragh had an unhealthy obsession with Jim Morrison and had this ridiculous idea that he wanted to die in his prime like Morrison, in his twenties, before he became middle-aged, fat and washed up. In the words of Neil Young, "It's better to burn out than to fade away."

Well, Darragh was 27 years old now, but Conor had thought that all that rubbish that he had spoken about not wanting to live beyond 27 was immature and drunken bullshit. He hadn't taken him seriously. Darragh was always babbling on about nonsense when he was drunk.

While Sarah was drying her eyes, there was a knock at the door. Conor answered it. It was a Guard, the same young Guard that had accompanied Detective Mulcahy into the house on the previous day. He was nervous and polite.

He took off his hat and asked if he could come in. "Ah, sorry to bother you both. Detective Mulcahy just radioed to tell me to ask you if you wouldn't mind going down to the Garda station in Castlederry to make an official statement as soon as you can."

"Sure, no problem. Has Darragh been located yet, do you know?" Conor asked.

"I'm sorry, I've heard nothing yet. I'm sure Jim—I mean Detective Mulcahy—will fill you in. I could run you down in the squad car, but unfortunately we have been told to wait here in case Mr Lonigan comes back. If you want, I can radio the station and they will have a car up here in twenty minutes to bring you to Castlederry," the young Guard said as he clenched his hands tightly around his hat.

"No, it's fine, I'll drive down in about an hour. Is that okay?" Sarah asked.

"Yes, yes, that's probably a better idea. You probably would prefer to travel in your own car and not in the back of a squad car. Okay, I'll radio ahead to say you'll be there in an hour or so," the Guard said as Conor closed the door.

"I wonder why they want us at the Garda station so soon," Sarah said to Conor.

"I suppose it's just routine. They just want to complete the paperwork, I imagine."

"Do you think they have found Darragh yet?" Sarah wondered.

"I dunno. I suppose they wouldn't be keeping that Garda car outside here if they had him in custody."

"What about that note I found in Darragh's coat pocket I found? Do you think I should show it to the Gardai in case it is some kind of suicide note?" Sarah asked as she read the note again.

"I suppose you should, if you're okay with them seeing it."

At around twelve midday, Sarah and Conor reached the Garda station in Castlederry. There were about twenty squad cars parked outside. The place looked extremely busy for a small-town Garda station. It showed how seriously the Gardai were taking the matter. The Castlederry station was the base for the entire operation.

Sarah decided to park her car down the street from the station and walk up to it. Conor and Sarah walked into the front door. They told the Ban Garda at the front desk that they wished to speak to Detective Mulcahy. The Ban Garda asked them who they were and as soon as they mentioned their names, she sprung to life and told them to follow her down the hallway into an office. She informed them that Detective Mulcahy would be with them in a few minutes.

Jim Mulcahy arrived into the office ten minutes later and apologised for keeping them waiting. He told them that he was just going to record their statements on a tape recorder so they would have an official record. They both agreed that it was okay.

Sarah tried to remain quiet and calm, but naturally, she had to ask, "Have you located Darragh yet?"

"No, Miss Gallagher, not yet. We have searched all of the properties that we know of that belong to the Lonigan family in the area. We called to the friends' home in Shemore that you told us about and we have checked all of the public houses that he usually frequented and nobody has seen him. We contacted his sister Anne in Strandhill and she informed us that he called to see her and his mother last Monday. They spent some time together and he informed them that he was planning to immigrate to Boston to make a 'fresh start', as he called it. He told his mother and sister that he was going to ask you, Sarah, to go with him and that he was going to contact your brother in Boston to find suitable accommodation over there.

"Darragh's mother told us that she had given him a substantial amount of money to pay for air fare and to help tide him over for a month or so in Boston until he found work and got established. She informed us that she gave him a cheque and so far, that cheque has not been cashed. Along with that, Darragh's sister lent him her car, a 1987 Silver Volkswagen Golf. He said he would return it to her as soon as he got his own car repaired at a garage."

"At this point, we haven't located the Golf. We have informed Gardai across the Republic about the car and we have also informed our good friends in the RUC in the North. The photographs that you gave to us have been photocopied and faxed to Garda stations across the country. Port authorities have also been notified to watch out for Mr Lonigan and the car."

"Now, perhaps he might have ditched the car because he realised that we might trace it to him, or he may have taken a ferry to Britain in the early hours of Tuesday morning. We have checked security cameras at the ports, but so far we haven't detected the Silver Golf. If we hear of anything else, we will let you know and naturally, if you can think of anything—it doesn't matter how trivial you might think it is—please pass it on to us. It might help to locate him."

Sarah reached into her handbag. "I found something, Detective. A note in a coat pocket that Darragh left behind him when he came back to the house on Tuesday morning. It might not be anything, but I was afraid that it could be a …" Sarah paused and began to cry. "A suicide note."

She handed the note across the desk to Jim Mulcahy. He reached into his pocket, pulled out a pair of reading glasses and proceeded to read the note. He put the note into an open file on the desk in front of him.

"Thank you, Sarah, for giving us such a personal item. It's hard to determine if it's a suicide note; it's quite vague. But we will have to, of course, consider this option. Did Darragh suffer from depression? Did he ever talk about matters such as suicide?" Detective Mulcahy asked.

"No, he was generally quite good humoured and easy going. He got a bit down from time to time, but no more than anybody else. I just thought that considering what has happened, maybe Darragh wasn't thinking straight," Sarah said.

"Well, as I said, Sarah, we will unfortunately have to consider this possibility," Detective Mulcahy replied.

Sarah and Conor were then brought to separate interviews rooms, where they were cross-examined about their knowledge of the events in question. After about an hour, they were allowed to leave and thanked for their cooperation.

Upon leaving the Garda station, the pair went to a pub up the street beside the space where they had parked the car. They had lunch and washed it down with a couple of stiff brandies to calm their nerves. They drove back to Ballinastrad and called into Maguire's shop to buy some groceries and two bottles of wine. From there, they headed back to the cottage in Rossbeg.

Chapter XIV

Dusk

Thursday, 5th January 1989

Conor woke up from the cold. He pulled the blankets up around his shoulders, but he couldn't warm himself.

Sarah was sleeping beside him in the bed. He looked at the clock; it was 8.30. He decided to get up and went over to the bedroom window to look outside to see what kind of day it was.

The place was gleaming white with a thick covering of snow that was still coming down heavy. He hadn't remarked that it was snowing when they went to bed the night before, but there it was.

After getting dressed, Conor walked into the freezing cold kitchen and decided to light the stove. There were no sticks in the wicker basket. He put on his coat to go outside to the shed at the side of the cottage to get fuel for the fire.

As he opened the front door, the view across to the Rossbeg Hills was breath-taking. The pure white snow made even the rough fields of rushes and whin bushes appear beautiful. It was a thick layer of snow; about four inches had fallen in a few short hours. The clouds overhead were still dark and heavy with the promise of more.

Conor noticed that the Garda car was still parked nearby and he felt sorry for the two Guards, who must have been freezing. He went over to the driver's window and tapped it. The Guard in the driver's seat rolled down the window.

"That was some fall of snow, lads. You must be freezing sitting there. Are you here all night?" Conor asked as he shivered.

"It's a heavy fall, all right. We're only here about two hours. Our shift started at seven o'clock, but it's cold enough, surely. The heater isn't great in this patrol car," the Guard replied in a strong Donegal accent.

"Look, it's not that warm in the house either. I'm just going to light the stove. Will you come in for a tea or coffee in half an hour when the heat builds up in the kitchen?"

"Sure, okay. That would be great, thanks," the Guard replied.

Conor turned around, went to the small shed and filled the large wicker basket he was carrying with some sticks and turf. He went back into the kitchen and got firelighters from the cupboard under the sink and lit the fire. He made some tea and toast for Sarah and himself and brought Sarah's breakfast down to her in the bedroom on a tray.

She was already awake and was getting dressed. He handed her the tray and she lay back to enjoy the treat of breakfast in bed. Afterwards, they both lay on the bed and they held each other tightly for warmth and for comfort. Both of them were afraid of what the next few days would bring.

"I'm due to fly back to England in two days' time. I have to be back at work in London the next Monday. But I don't know what to do. I feel bad leaving you to face all of this nightmare alone. I think I'll contact a travel agent to see if I could defer the flight for an extra few days. I'll have to arrange further leave from work, too," Conor said.

"You don't have to do that, Conor. I'll be okay. I'm going to move out of here as soon as I can. The cottage belongs to Darragh's family. They won't want me staying here now."

"Where will you go? I'm sure you could stay here for a few more months."

"No, I want to get out of here as quickly as possible. I might rent an apartment in Ballygalvin. It would be handy for work. Maybe I should just go over to my brother in Boston. Myself and Darragh had planned to immigrate, you know. We saved up the money in the spring of last year, but Darragh changed his mind. He got cold feet and decided that he didn't want to go. He never really explained why. Instead, we blew the money we had saved on a holiday in Scotland."

"What about your job?" Conor asked.

"I'm sick of that fucking bank. I'm sick of this whole fucking place. Oh, I'm sorry, Conor. I don't know really what I want. I can't think straight."

"It's okay, Sarah. Look, I meant to tell you that it is snowing heavy outside and I felt sorry for the two Guards in the squad car. I invited them in to warm themselves by the fire."

"Look, I don't feel very sociable. You can entertain them. I think I will soak in a warm bath for a while to try to get my head together."

The stove in the kitchen was blazing and the room was getting warmer when Conor returned from the bedroom. There was a knock at the door. Conor opened it. One of the Guards stood outside.

"Come in, sorry. I was just about to call you in," Conor said as he stepped back to let the Guard in.

"Thanks very much, Conor, for your offer, but unfortunately we have to leave. We just thought we would let you know that we were just radioed that a silver Golf that matches the description of the one that Darragh Lonigan was last seen driving has been located in a wooded area not too far from here. We have got our orders to go there, as we are the nearest patrol car to the location. Another Garda car may be sent here shortly to take our place," the Guard said.

"Oh, right. What? Where? Whereabouts? Which wooded area?" Conor was shocked.

"We were told that if you turn right outside the house here and keep on this lane for two miles, there is a crossroads at Shemore Church. You take a left and travel on there for about a mile and that brings you to a large forest called Dunmadden Woods, I think. Does that sound familiar to you?" the Guard asked.

"I'm not that familiar with the area around here, to be honest," Conor replied.

"Okay, look. Thanks for the offer for the tea, but we better be off. I just thought I would let you know. We will keep you informed if it turns out to be the car we are looking for."

When Conor passed on the information to Sarah, they immediately decided to travel down to Dunmadden Woods to see if it was true.

"Do you know where the woods are, Sarah and how to get there?"

"I know those woods very well. Myself and Darragh often went there for walks around that area. He loved that place; it is about two miles away from a sandy shore of Lough Oughter where we used to go swimming on warm summer days. During the wintertime, Darragh would often go there as well to just stare at the lake. He said it had a calming effect on him."

As she told Conor, she suddenly burst into tears. "Oh God, why did he leave the car there? Where is he? Do you think he might have…?"

Conor tried to console her. "Look, firstly, it might not be the car he was driving. Or maybe if it was the car, he might just have broken down and left it there."

He was finding it hard to convince himself, never mind Sarah. Like her, he was thinking the worst.

The snow was falling heavy outside as they left the cottage and went out into the yard. Conor cleaned the heavy coating of snow that covered Sarah's car with a brush. He insisted that he would drive because Sarah was so upset.

He started the car and put the heater on to try to clear the windscreen. It took nearly ten minutes before they could see out through it. During that time, Sarah just stared blankly at the windscreen; she was too consumed by her own thoughts to respond when Conor tried to speak to her. He couldn't find the right words to say anyway.

Finally, Conor was able to drive the car out of the yard and onto the narrow road. The wheels spun as he tried to get traction to climb the slight rise onto the road. The journey was going to be difficult in more ways than one.

The hills around Rossbeg proved a challenge for the Ford Mondeo. Fortunately, it appeared that other vehicles had travelled the route earlier; they had cut a path through the heavy snow.

Conor was too transfixed in his own thoughts to notice the brilliant white winter scene around him. He kept hoping that maybe Darragh had ditched the car in the woods and travelled on somewhere else. He kept hoping for impossible outcomes.

He hoped that the confession that Darragh had made to him in the hotel in Galway was just drunken ramblings from a very intoxicated man. He hoped that there was no proof to link Darragh to the murder of Tom Kearns. That it was all a big mix up, a misunderstanding. He hoped that Darragh was somewhere else far away, maybe standing at a bar, laughing and joking, being cool, confident, and happy. That's the way Conor wanted to picture him.

However, he knew that this was just an idle fantasy. The reality was too hard to handle. Was Darragh lying cold, lifeless and alone somewhere in deep Lough Oughter, or within the dark and grey, leafless trees of Dunmadden Woods?

Conor drove on slowly and carefully even though he was eager to reach Dunmadden to see if the Guard's information was true. The window wipers were battling hard to keep the heavy falling snow at bay. Eventually, he reached the church at Shemore and from there, Sarah directed him to take a sharp left at a junction down a very narrow lane that would bring them to the woods and beyond that, Lough Oughter.

The lane showed little evidence of previous travel by cars that morning. Driving the Mondeo was proving even more difficult as Conor navigated endless tight corners and steep hills. In the end, the car could go no further, as the wheels spun, unable to get a grip on a hill that felt like a mountain.

Conor made several attempts to get up it by reversing back down and trying to build up speed to climb. They were only about a third of a mile from their destination, so instead of continuing to try, Conor and Sarah decided to pull the car off the road and into a gateway beside a field and make the remaining part of their journey on foot.

The pair got out of the car and wrapped their coats tightly around them as they faced the blowing wind and bitter flakes of snow. Conor held his arm around Sarah's shoulder to support her as they walked up the hill. From the top of it, they could see a large wooded area, maybe forty acres of forested land.

"It's a very old wood planted by a Lord Dunmadden back in the mid-nineteenth century. He was the local landlord in the area. Local people say that it was planted to cover a Famine mass grave and that there could be thousands of poor souls buried under those tall oaks," Sarah told Conor as they walked towards the woods. "If you look over to the right of the woods, you can see Lough Oughter. It's the largest lake in the county. I think I read that it is twelve miles long and at its widest point, it's four miles. It attracts anglers from all over the country and from overseas."

Conor heard a vehicle coming up behind them. He looked back to see a grey Range Rover. It drove towards them and stopped. The window on the passenger's side was rolled down. Conor recognised the face inside; it was Detective Jim Mulcahy.

"You shouldn't be up here. Is that your car back there, the Ford Mondeo? Is it broken down?" Jim asked bluntly.

"No, just couldn't get any further," Conor replied.

"You really should stay back at home until we find out who this car belongs to. Look, get in the back of the jeep, it's bloody freezing out there," Jim said as he got out to open the doors of the Range Rover to let Sarah and Conor in.

"Did you find the car that Darragh was driving?" Conor asked Jim.

"We found a silver Golf."

"How long was it there?" Sarah asked.

"It was discovered there yesterday morning by three men who arrived to cut timber. The car was parked in the middle of the pass that was the main access into the woods where they had been cutting timber for the last few months. At first, they didn't really pass much remarks on it. They thought it could just belong to somebody out for a walk around the woods or lake, as many people walk around there, especially this week, as people are still on Christmas holidays. However, they noticed that the car was still there yesterday evening when they finished work and were coming out of the woods about five o'clock and it hadn't moved this morning at 8.30 when they came back. Obviously, this made them suspicious."

"Was the car locked?" Conor asked.

"The workmen went over to look at the car and noticed that it wasn't locked and the keys were still in the ignition. At that point, one of the men went up to the phone box beside Shemore Church and contacted us. Garda Ryan and Garda McLoughlin went straight to the scene about half an hour ago. They were the two Guards that were at the checkpoint outside Sarah's home. That's as much as we know so far," Jim responded.

The Range Rover came to the junction and turned left down a rough, wet pass, which was the entrance into Dunmadden Woods. About a mile along the pass, the vehicle came to a stop. In front of them was a Garda patrol car and in front of that was the silver Volkswagen Golf.

Detective Mulcahy went over to the car where Garda Ryan and McLoughlin were examining it. He immediately looked at the number plates and checked them against the car registration given to him by Darragh's sister, Anne. They must've matched, because Conor could see him nodding. The detective went over to the two young Guards and Conor strained to listen in.

"Well, it's the car all right. Have you found anything of interest in or around the car yet?" Jim Mulcahy asked as he opened the car door and peered inside.

"No, nothing yet, Detective Mulcahy. I'm afraid we only just got here about five minutes ago. We got it tight to get up some of those bloody hills with the feckin' snow." Garda McLoughlin replied in that rough Donegal accent.

"What does it look like to you, lads? If it's a suicide, it's going to be some job locating the body in these woods in this weather. If he is in the lake, that's a whole different story. We are going to need a hell of a lot more manpower to find the remains."

Jim Mulcahy returned to the range Rover to talk to Sarah and Conor.

"Well, the car does belong to Darragh's sister and presumably Darragh parked it there early on Tuesday morning. Where he went after that obviously is unknown at present."

"What happens now?" Conor asked.

"What happens now is that I plan to organise a thorough search of the area as soon as sufficient resources are made available."

The detective didn't spell it out to Sarah and Conor, but the logical follow on was that Darragh must have taken his life somewhere in the vicinity.

"Do ye want a lift back to your car?"

Sarah didn't answer. She seemed numb; she sat motionless and stared at the Golf and the dark woods surrounding it, which were coated in a canopy of white snow.

"We're okay, thanks. I think that we would prefer to walk back to clear our heads a bit. It's a lot to take in," Conor replied.

"Okay, I'll be in touch if we discover … I'll call up to the house or send one of the Guards if there are any developments."

"I'd like to give some help with the search. If you need help?" Conor asked.

"Yea, Conor, I appreciate that. I'll let you know if we need you."

The couple got out of the back seat of the jeep. The snow had stopped falling and was turning into a light sleety rain.

"Let's walk down towards the lake shore for a few minutes, Conor."

"Okay, Sarah, if it makes you feel better."

Conor held Sarah's hand and they turned out from the woods and walked down the snow-covered path to Lough Oughter, a path that she had taken with Darragh many, many times. When they reached the shore, Sarah stood for ten minutes surveying the lake and the snow-covered hills that surrounded it. It was if she could sense that the spirit of Darragh was resting there.

Conor held her tightly with his arm around her shoulder. Her long black mane was blowing around her face. Tears were streaming down her cheeks, but he thought he noticed a small smile appear on her face and a calmness come over her. She turned and looked at Conor and said, "I'm okay now. Let's go."

They returned to Sarah's car, which they had parked at the base of the steep hill leading to the woods. Conor turned the car around and headed back to the cottage.

Sarah was quiet, but her tears had ceased and she appeared unusually calm and content. It was as if she had reached a point of acceptance that Darragh was gone and she must try to remember him for who he was. Despite the fact that he had been unfaithful to her countless times, she knew that he had loved her and they had spent so many happy days together. She believed that he was at peace now.

They arrived back at the cottage and Sarah immediately busied herself by putting more sticks in the stove and preparing lunch. Conor was amazed at how her mood had changed; he still felt devastated about what had happened. He had tried to be the strong one over the last two days, but now it appeared the roles had dramatically reversed.

"I think that it's time to move on, Conor, to leave the cottage and start again. I'm going to spend the rest of the day packing most of my things and then ring Roisin Sheridan to see if she would put me up for a few nights until I can find a place of my own."

"I'm sure you could stay here for a few months, Sarah. What's the rush?"

"I've made up my mind. I don't want to stay in this cottage anymore. There are too many memories and anyway, with Darragh gone, the Lonigan family would probably want me out."

"Well, maybe you're right. I'll help you to pack."

Conor helped Sarah to put her possessions into cardboard boxes and bin bags. All around the cottage were sketchbooks belonging to Darragh full of rough ideas for paintings. These paintings would never now be completed. There was a wardrobe full of his clothes and a large record and cassette collection was stacked in the corner of the bedroom.

After two hours of packing, Sarah drove down to the phone box at the local post office and rang her friend Roisin to ask if she could stay with her for a few nights. Roisin told her it was no problem and to come over that evening.

Conor was again taken aback at how quickly she was moving out. It obviously meant that they would not be spending another night together in the cottage. He was unsure what to think of that. Was Sarah now ashamed of what had happened between them? Did she just want to forget about it, to get on with her life and make a brand new start? Perhaps the only way Sarah could deal with the pain now was to keep busy. Maybe it was a coping mechanism. Conor was just relieved that she wouldn't be spending time alone in the cottage.

He would be going back to England shortly anyway. If Darragh's remains were found around Lough Oughter over the next forty-eight hours, though, he obviously wanted to remain in Ballinastrad for the funeral, whenever that would be arranged.

After making the phone call to Roisin, the pair returned to the cottage. They carried Sarah's belongings out to the car and packed the boot and backseat. As Sarah went out the door of the kitchen, she looked behind her. To take in the scene for a few moments, Conor assumed. Then she switched off the lights and locked the door.

She drove Conor into Ballinastrad and dropped him outside his parents' house.

"Look, thanks, Conor, for everything today and for the last few days. I wouldn't have gotten through this without you. I just need to get away from here for a while. I can't stay in the cottage anymore—too many ghosts. I hope you understand."

"Yea, I understand, Sarah. Well, I think I do. It's all so fucked up I don't know what to do or think anymore. It's all so fucking hard to take in and make sense of. In some ways, it doesn't feel bloody real," Conor said angrily as he stared out the windscreen.

"I hope you will be okay, Conor. Look, here is the phone number of the house I am staying at. Give me a ring tomorrow and we will arrange something," Sarah said, writing the number on the back of a cigarette box and handing it to Conor.

"Okay, look, I'll let you get on. I'll ring you so tomorrow," Conor said as he kissed Sarah on the lips and got out of the car. He watched her drive out the Castlederry road and then he turned to look up the quiet main street of Ballinastrad and across to Sheehan's Pub.

He decided that he needed a pint very badly.

Chapter XV

April Skies

Tuesday, 18th April 1989

(Three Months Later)

London

Conor climbed the three flights of stairs carrying a bag of shopping. His black coat was soaking wet and heavy as he fumbled in his pocket to find the keys to his apartment. He opened the apartment door and went in, closing the door behind him with his foot.

The wet bag of groceries was thrown up on the worktop in the kitchen as he took off the coat and placed it on the back of a chair next to the kitchen table. In the bedroom, he took off the remainder of his wet clothes and put on an old t-shirt, jeans and a pair of runners. The sound of double-decker buses rumbled outside. Looking through his window at the streets of Kilburn below, Conor could see hundreds of people shuffling through the wet streets and trying to get on buses or in taxis to escape the rain and get home.

As he went back into the small kitchen, he turned on the central heating and grabbed a large red apple from a bowl on the worktop. He flopped down on the couch in the living room and grabbed the remote, flicking through a few TV channels until he came across a documentary on BBC2. Staring at the image of Lake Victoria in central Africa on the screen, his mind drifted to another lake back home in Sligo.

Conor had been back in London now for just over three months. The search for Darragh had begun immediately the day the car was discovered in Dunmadden Woods. Gardai had been drafted in from all over the county to search the area.

The wintry conditions had made the search almost impossible. The heavy snow had lasted for three days and had been followed by a severe frost that had lasted a further week. As temperatures had slowly increased, a thaw had come, resulting in flooding for a number of days as the snow and ice melted. The days had also been so short, with only about nine hours of January daylight from a low winter sun that never really fully penetrated the dark interior of the woods.

The Gardai, Civil Defence and members of the general public had combed the woods in search of some trace of Darragh. The woods were vast and trying to walk through the thick undergrowth had been a challenge in itself. Conor, along with many of his friends and neighbours, had helped in the search for a week. He had been due back at work in London on Monday the 9th of January, but he'd managed to get an extra week off. Detective Jim Mulcahy had focussed on searching the woods during the first week because

145

Lough Oughter had been frozen in parts, with a thick layer of ice that had made searches of it futile.

As Conor had searched through Dunmadden Woods, one part of him had hoped that he would find Darragh's remains so that his friend could be given a proper burial. Another part of him had been horrified at the thought of discovering him hanging from a tree or finding him lying in a wet drain after taking an overdose or freezing to death from hypothermia.

As Conor thought about Darragh, he also thought about Sarah. He had never rung Sarah back the day after she had moved out of the cottage as he had promised to. He'd thought it was probably best to leave her to herself to make a new life and a new start. He assumed that she was still working at the bank in Ballygalvin and living with her friend, or that she maybe had the apartment of her own that she had been planning to get. Possibly she had taken the plunge and immigrated to be with her brother in Boston.

Conor often thought about her. In fact, most days he thought about what might have happened if things had worked out differently for them. He realised, though, that it was probably best just to try to put it behind him and move on.

After the end of the first week of searching, Conor had returned to London. He was now kept informed of developments by regular telephone conversations with his parents. His father had told him that a few days after he had returned to England, the thaw came and the ice melted on Lough Oughter. This resulted in scuba diving teams from all over western Ireland being drafted in to begin an extensive search of the lake. However, the sheer size and depth of the body of water made searching its murky waters extremely difficult.

The Guards hoped that once the ice melted on the lake surface, Darragh's body, if it was in there, would rise to the surface and be spotted with the aid of a helicopter as it flew low overhead. The thaw had made diving easier; however, the melting snows on the hills of Rossbeg that surrounded Lough Oughter had begun to release floods of water into the lake which intensified its already fast-moving currents. Tree branches and other debris had begun to move, which had hampered the search effort. Lough Oughter also was drained by a series of rivers, which meant that if Darragh's remains were in the lake, they could be quickly washed many miles away by the fast-moving currents as the volume of water in the lake rapidly increased.

Lough Oughter was vast. If Darragh's body didn't come to the surface itself, the resultant search of the depths of the lake would be a titanic task. After three weeks of intensive trawling of the lake waters, the search had been moved to the rivers that drained the Lough.

By the first week of February, a month since Darragh had gone missing, the search had been scaled down. Garda resources were needed elsewhere.

Darragh's body was never found. It could have been washed many miles away by the flooded lake currents into the numerous local rivers that were tributaries of the River Moy, which ran through Counties Sligo and Mayo.

And that was if the body was ever in Lough Oughter. At times, Conor often wondered if Darragh had staged the whole thing. Had he written the supposed suicide note for Sarah and parked his sister's car in Dunmadden Woods near the shore of Lough Oughter to make it look like a suicide? Had Darragh faked his own suicide so that he could move to some other place and start life again under a different name without worrying about the Gardai constantly hunting him? He had no passport, so he couldn't have travelled to the USA. Was he alive and well somewhere in Ireland or Britain or on the Continent?

However, the more Conor thought about it, the more it seemed highly unlikely. The silver Golf had a half tank of diesel. It had started with a turn of the ignition when checked by Detective Mulcahy. It hadn't broken down. It had had no flat tyres. So why would Darragh leave a car in the middle of nowhere unless he was planning to kill himself? Perhaps Conor wanted to believe that his old friend was still alive somewhere because it was an easier thought to deal with than picturing his bloated body floating in a watery grave.

Conor felt very guilty for what had happened. What if he had gone to the Garda station in Galway City and informed them of Darragh's confession to him straight away on the 2nd of January? Then, perhaps, Darragh would have been arrested and would still be alive today, if in Garda custody awaiting trial.

What if he hadn't been in bed with Sarah in the cottage in Rossbeg when Darragh returned and discovered them? Then Darragh's suicide might never have happened.

What if Darragh had one more pint that night, the 21st of December, in Sheehan's Pub in Ballinastrad? Then perhaps Tom Kearns might have got a lift home with somebody else and he wouldn't have been walking on the Rossbeg road when Darragh was driving home.

What if Darragh hadn't driven home drunk and hit Tom and left him dying on the road? What if, instead of driving off and leaving Tom Kearns bleeding to death, he had done the proper thing and gone to a nearby house to ring for an ambulance?

But they were all just big 'what ifs'.

Conor had rung his parents at the weekend gone by to check for any developments at home. His father had told him that the Gardai had more or less stopped searching now. It had been over three months since Darragh had disappeared and his body might never be found at this stage.

Conor told his parents that he would try to get home for a holiday in the summer, maybe in August. He missed his parents and looked forward to seeing them, but the thoughts of returning to Ballinastrad did not appeal to him now.

Hunger pangs came over Conor and he decided to cook himself a meal, something quick and handy, as he was wrecked after a long day at work and he still wasn't sleeping that well at night. The culinary delight that was scrambled eggs on toast was brought over to the coffee table and eaten in front of the TV. After eating, he flicked over the channels again and found a football game to watch. About twenty minutes later, Conor was snoozing, even though it was just quarter to nine.

A knock at the door woke him up. At first, he ignored it, but then a second knock rapped on the door.

He got up from the couch, walked towards the door, and opened it. He wasn't expecting any callers. Maybe it was one of the lads from Longford who lived in the flat downstairs; they dropped in for a chat some evenings.

"Hi, Conor," a female voice said.

It was Sarah.

Conor couldn't quite believe it. His mouth dropped open and he found it difficult to respond.

"Hi. Hi, Sarah. God, I wasn't expecting to see you," he said.

"Some Irish guy let me in as he was going out downstairs. I asked him which apartment you were in and

149

he told me. I got the address of the house from your mother. I met her in the bank in Ballygalvin a few weeks ago and I asked her for it and she gave it to me. I said I was going to write to you."

"Come in. Let me give you a hand with that bag," Conor said as he lifted the large rucksack that was on the floor next to Sarah. He was still in a state of shock and couldn't quite believe that she was there in the apartment. He was dumbfounded and felt awkward. There was so much he wanted to say to her, but he was unable to speak.

Sarah was soaking wet from the heavy rain outside. Conor gave her a towel to dry her hair and asked her if she had dry clothes in her rucksack to put on. She said she had, and she went into the bathroom to change. Conor hung her wet clothes beside the radiators.

He brought a half bottle of whiskey from the cupboard over the sink to warm Sarah up from her soaking. As the drink went down, the conversation flowed more easily.

"Well, Sarah, how's things going back in Sligo? To ask a stupid question, why are you in London on a wet Tuesday night?" Conor asked as he laughed.

"I packed up the job at the bank last week. I was sick of it. I just couldn't settle in Ballygalvin. I had to get away. To get away from Sligo, get away from Ireland. I want to travel and I thought that London could be a good base to start from."

"Well, good for you, Sarah. God, I'd love to travel. You're lucky you have the freedom to do it."

"What's stopping you from travelling? Why don't you come with me? We could go to India or Nepal and live with Buddhist monks." Sarah laughed.

"Maybe I will, who knows?"

The pair spoke for hours and they laughed as they retold old stories about their adventures in Galway while in university back in the early years of the decade. They were the happy times they wanted to remember, the happy memories of themselves and Darragh. Later, Sarah's laughter turned to tears and as Sarah cried, Conor reached out to hold her. As he held her, she kissed him and told him that the real reason she came to London was not to travel, but to be with him.

Conor and Sarah lay together in bed that night and held each other close. As they slept, they dreamt of the lonely hills of Rossbeg and the now empty cottage. They imagined the grey woods of Dunmadden and the nearby sandy shore of Lough Oughter and the stars and the whole of the moon shining down upon it on a cool April night. The light breeze crossing through the young fragile leaves on the trees in the woods and the gentle ripple of the water on the surface of the lake as the soft breeze passed over … and then there was silence.